Minister Debbie Reid

Penned for Purpose
Publishing
Charlotte, North Carolina

All scriptures quoted are from the New Living Translation of the Bible unless otherwise noted.

Life Ever Altered

ISBN: 979-8-9868965-1-9

Copyright © 2022 Min. Debbie Reid
All publishing rights belong exclusively to Penned for Purpose Publishing

Cover Design – Kenya Gould, Designs By Kenya, kenya@designsbykenya.com

Printed in the United States of America

Dedication

This book is dedicated to those who have experienced false accusations, those who others have turned their backs on. Remember, God has the final say, and He has a marvelous way of turning things around for His children!

Titles By This Author

Shedding Silent Tears – Inspirational Fiction

"I haven't read or even had the desire to read a book for years. I looked for a book title matching my own emotions. I started page one...every possibility I 'made' possible...I read. There are so many similar feelings and circumstances I can relate to. For years, I also thought I was alone in the world. Believe it or not, this book made me stand up for myself and many things that have been bothering me for decades. And I have... It's very hard, but when I do...I feel better about it. One day at a time.... Thanks, Debbie"

Train Our Hands to War – Christian

"I loved the wisdom within the pages of the book. The prayers are timeless and powerful. I found myself praying for them over my own life, and they are written in a way that I could add my own words along with the words shared by the author. I particularly liked the different spin on the breakdown of the Lord's Prayer. I can see this being a great resource to remind us that God is always with us, even in our toughest situations. Strongly recommend!"

Chapter 1

evon was in disbelief over his current predicament. He looked around the interrogation room, entirely beside himself. He pondered for almost an hour, "How could anyone possibly think I could be capable of murder?" Devon's clammy hands were pressed against his face as his mind continued spiraling uncontrollably. He could not fathom why the police needed him to come to the police department but vowed to get to the bottom of it.

Detective Sneed was one of two Detectives who finally entered the room. Neither one bothered to introduce themselves, but Devon saw their last names on their name tags. Sneed was the heavier set of the two and stood roughly five feet eight with a physique appearing to have once been muscular. The muscles are now replaced by sagging arms and a protruding stomach. He carried a grimace on his pale reddish face. His legs seemed short and stocky, but he had no problem whisking around the room. This was evident as he repeatedly paced the breadth of the room. He ran his chubby fingers through his balding brown hair showing apparent frustration. Devon figured this was either an intimidation tactic or something more daunting was troubling this man. Whichever it was, it made his countenance seem unsettled. Devon watched closely, preparing himself for the worst while praying for the best. As a Black man sitting in an interrogation room, he knew he needed to be respectful; however, he struggled not to be caught off guard. He thought back to the talk his father had with him when he was younger and heard his voice as stern and adamantly as though he were present, "Keep both hands in plain sight. No movements without asking permission. Maintain a confident but not intimidating stance and hold your tongue so you can return home to us unharmed."

The second gentleman, Detective Johnston, was a bit calmer in his overall demeanor but an intimidating presence, nonetheless. He was approximately four inches taller than his counterpart, which put him at roughly six feet tall. He appeared much younger, maybe in his mid-thirties, whereas Detective Sneed had to be closer to sixty. Detective Johnston had a chiseled frame. He could have easily been a football player in his youth. His arms were well defined—massive, as a matter of fact, rippling through his short-sleeved dress shirt. He had a substantial upper frame tapering down to a trim waistline and what could easily be six-pack abs. His legs were also muscular, rippling even through his uniform pants. He had a deep tan and a slight British accent.

"Pastor Royce...answer the question!" exclaimed an agitated Detective Sneed as he stopped pacing and plopped down into a chair across from Devon. His massiveness crowded Devon's personal space.

"I'm sorry. Can you repeat the question again?" Devon asked, snapping out of his fog.

"Pastor Royce," Detective Johnston repeated in a calmer voice, "Look at the pictures. How do you know this woman?" Devon identified the good-cop-bad cop routine they were enacting, yet he knew he dared not test either of them.

Devon diverted his attention to the scratched, scraped wooden table before him. Certainly, it had seen its fair share of interrogations, as was evident by the carving of initials, vulgar words, and deeply drawn lines. In front of him were markings that seemed to result from metal handcuffs rubbing against the table's surface. Devon surmised that many people who were presumed guilty sat in this same room even before they had a chance to prove their innocence. On the table was an open plain manila folder displaying gruesome, graphic photographs of a young woman from various angles whose face and body were brutally beaten and unrecognizable. In one of the more disturbing photos, the young lady lay in a pool of blood with a gunshot wound to her stomach. Her eyes were still open and seemed to pierce through Devon's soul.

"Detective, as I said before, I have no idea who this woman is," Devon insisted. "Her face is brutally battered and mangled. It would be hard for anyone to identify her. I feel horrible for her and her family and will certainly keep them in my thoughts and prayers, but I cannot say that I know her."

"What if I told you we have eyewitnesses?" Detective Sneed barked as he banged his fist on the table, clearly trying to exude his authority.

"If you have eyewitnesses, why am I here? Shouldn't you go after the person who did this to that poor woman?"

"*Pastor...* Royce," Detective Sneed emphasized sarcastically, smirking at the mere thought of calling this potential criminal a pastor. "You know, this looks bad for you. If you are found guilty, you could land in prison for twenty years." Why don't you cooperate with us and maybe, just maybe, we can help you negotiate a lesser charge? What if I told you the eyewitnesses identified you as the perpetrator?"

Pastor Devon was visibly shaken. Beads of sweat began traveling from his forehead and landing on the collar of his shirt. "Twenty years! No way! Why would anyone think it was me?"

"Can you detail where you were yesterday evening?" Detective Johnston probed.

"I was at my church until about 9:00 p.m. I had a lot on my mind, so when I left, I took a drive to clear my head before heading home. It was a stressful day, more so than normal." Devon began as he grimaced, recalling the encounter with a stranger at the church. He paused before continuing. "I don't like to take matters of the church home to my family, so I drove around the city to clear my head and speak with the Lord before going home. Something I typically do."

"Interesting! Is there anyone who can confirm your story other than the Lord, of course?" Sneed again with his sarcasm. He may have been playing a role, but something told Devon it was more than an act. This man seemed as if he had demons he was fighting. He was clearly unsettled in his spirit. He made a mental note to add Detective Sneed to his prayer list. Even though Sneed was rude and angry, it had more to do with what was plaguing him and less to do with the good pastor.

"What time did you get to the church, Pastor Royce?" Johnston chimed in.

"I was with my family from the time I got up until–hmmm–I guess about 6:00 p.m. We are quite intentional about having family time every Thursday during the spring and summer. I took them to Carowinds and out to dinner," Devon responded. "As we were eating, I received a call from Deacon Maurice. We quickly wrapped up our meal and headed home. After I dropped my family at home, I made my way to the church. Several people were there who could confirm my whereabouts. As a matter of fact, the choir was rehearsing. I remember popping my head in to say hello when I got in."

"But if the choir was rehearsing, the members couldn't possibly know when you arrived and departed the church. Isn't that right, Pastor Royce?" Sneed interjected.

15

"I guess not, but the church administrator, Angelique, and Brother Lucas were also there. Deacon Maurice was the one who called me, so of course, he was present as well. They were all in Angelique's office. There was a young lady I counseled with, which was why I was called in that night in the first place. In fact, Deacon Maurice walked me to my car as we wrapped up our business."

"So, what was so urgent that Deacon Maurice had to pull you away from your family?"

Devon paused as he looked from one Detective to the other. "There was someone who had come to the church who needed counseling."

"Who was the - someone, and what type of counseling?"

"I cannot divulge the details of the counseling session with you, but she was not a member of our church. She was in a panicked state, and Sister Angelique and Deacon Maurice thought it best that I come in to speak with her."

"Ok, so maybe you have an alibi up until you left the church, but who can vouch for you taking a drive to clear your head, and what time did you return home?" asked Johnston.

"Of course, no one was in the car with me, and I didn't have a particular destination. I hear God's voice most clearly while driving, and last night, I needed to hear from Him. I guess I don't have anyone who could vouch for me during that time."

"And you got home at what time?" Johnston asked, taking over the interrogation. He sensed a wave of unsettling anger rising from his partner and thought it better for him to add a bit more professionalism to the interview. Being Detective Sneed's partner for two years, he knew when his partner was playing a role and when something within his own life caused him to lash out at others. It was not the best look for the police, given the current social climate and racial unrest. A White cop losing it on a Black pastor would not bode well for either race.

"I don't know exactly, maybe about 11:30 p.m. I don't understand this. I cannot fathom why anyone would claim I was anywhere near wherever this young lady died."

"How would you know? We didn't tell you where she was *murdered,* so maybe you were in the proximity," Sneed chimed in, emphasizing the word murdered, trying to further ruffle Devon's feathers and possibly catch him in a lie. It was clear he needed to exude some level of authority.

"Man, if it did not happen on the highway, I was not there," responded an agitated Devon. "I shouldn't say anything more until I consult with my attorney!"

"If you aren't guilty, why do you need an attorney, Pastor Royce?" Sneed inquired.

"Because it is my right to have legal representation. Surely you will not deny me my rights, would you, Detective Sneed? I will not say anything more without my attorney present."

Sneed turned blood red as his body tightened even more. It was clear Devon had pushed one button too many with him. Seeing this, Detective Johnston intervened, "You are correct. It is your right to have legal representation, but I believe this meeting is over for now. Technically, we cannot keep you here. You are not under arrest, but I would strongly suggest you reach out to that attorney of yours and make sure you do not leave the city."

"Stay here. We will be right back," Detective Johnston replied. He and his partner left the interrogation room and entered an adjacent room occupied by their lead Detective, Joe Ramsey. They could see Pastor Devon through the two-way mirror in the room. After watching him for a moment, Detective Ramsey turned to Detectives Sneed and Johnston, "So what are you thinking?"

With teeth clenched, Officer Sneed demanded, "Get the paperwork started for an expedited search warrant for his home and church office! There is more to Devon Royce than meets the eye."

"Sneed!" Detective Ramsey reprimanded. "Let's not forget I am your superior. You need to watch how you address me. I watched you during the interview; if you are dealing with personal issues, you need to deal with them outside of here. I will not tolerate any of my men abusing civilians, innocent or otherwise. Do I make myself clear?"

"Yes, sir," a deflated Detective Sneed replied. "You are right; I should not bring my personal issues to the job."

"We can discuss you taking some personal time, but for now, do you really believe he had something to do with this?"

"You bet your boots I do! And we are going to find out just what his involvement is!"

"What about you, Johnston? Do you agree with your partner?"

"It's too early to tell, but I believe he may know more than he is admitting."

Nodding his head slowly as if to process what the detectives just shared, Detective Ramsey responded, "Ok, well, let's get the search warrant, gentlemen. But for now, let him go."

Chapter 2

*D*aria Hendrix-Royce was beyond shaken when her husband was escorted out of their home by the boys in blue. Devon Royce was a muscular, wildly attractive bag of chocolate goodness who stood six feet two with a silky complexion. At least, that is how Daria saw her husband. She remembered the first day she felt the spark all women dreamed of feeling toward a man. The spark where the attraction was more than physical; the mental stimulation was intense, and the reciprocation was evident. Next to God, Devon was the best thing to ever happen to her.

He was the moon to her stars. He was not only her love and the father of her children; they were best friends. They enjoyed spending time together. Even when they argued, as most couples do, they would not stay upset long because it would keep them apart, something neither of them could handle for more than a couple of hours.

Daria could not believe how quickly their day had shifted. Just hours before, she and Devon were lying in bed laughing and loving one another, and now her *moon,* her beloved husband, was sitting in the back of a police car. Daria literally felt the light dim in her spirit. She did not know what could have possibly happened to cause the police to come knocking on their door at 8:30 a.m.

on a Friday morning. They asked some simple questions while they stood at the door but, for whatever reason, felt the need to take him down to the station. She knew Devon could not be involved in any crime, but why else would they take him? Did he witness a crime and not tell her? Did something terrible happen at the church? The Detectives were not forthcoming with information, though they did not hesitate to escort him out of their home and down their driveway.

Still, Daria could not fully digest the sight of them putting Devon in the back of their police car. Fortunately, they did not handcuff him, so she knew he was not under arrest, at least not officially, anyway. She had angst with the situation as she knew the Charlotte Police Department did not have the best record regarding interactions with Black and Brown people. A few years prior, there were televised incidents of protests, riots, and violence after a police Detective shot and killed Keith Lamont Scott while attempting to serve a warrant to someone else. Her mind raced to other instances of Black and Brown men and women across the country who lost their lives at the hands of the police: *Daunte Wright, Andre Hill, George Floyd, Breonna Taylor, Philando Castile, Alton Sterling, Freddie Gray, Eric Garner, Tamir Rice, Michael Brown, Tyre Nichols* and so many others. Tears gushed from her eyes as she thought of the 'Say My Name' protests. She could not bear to think of her husband being next on that list.

Once the vehicles were out of sight, Daria closed the door and leaned with her back against it. Thoughts ravaged her mind. She struggled to stay focused and be courageous for Devon and their children. Her children!

She instantly snapped back to reality. It was just after 8:30 a.m. when the Detectives interrupted their morning. Daria went upstairs to check on her babies, hoping they were still fast asleep and praying they did not see their dad taken away by the police. They were too young and impressionable. Daria was in shock, so she could not imagine how their little minds would process the situation.

She enjoyed watching her babies nestled in their beds: Nina, the oldest, was now eleven years old. She was such an intelligent young lady and had the wisdom of her ancestors. It was amazing to watch her evolve as she entered her preteen years. Where had the time gone? Daria pondered as she went in to wake her.

"What's going on, Mommy? Nina asked in a groggy tone. "I heard someone at the door."

"Nothing, baby. Just some business Daddy had to take care of. Forget all of that. I have a surprise for you?"

"A surprise? What is it?" Nina quickly adjusted herself on her bed; her big brown eyes glowed more radiant than ever. Daria always marveled at how much Nina looked like Devon. Her facial features mirrored those of her father. She was lanky, a little more than average height for her age, with a medium brown complexion. She had natural black hair twisted into beautiful ponytails that hung well below her shoulders.

"You guys are going to go with Auntie Tasha to Virginia."

"Really, Mommy?"

"Yes. We decided it would be good for you to spend time with her, then she will take you to your grandparents for a couple of weeks."

"Yaaay!"

"So, get dressed and get your clothes in your suitcase while I wake up your brother and sister.

"Ok, Mommy."

Nina loved her Auntie Tasha and was always overjoyed about spending time with her grandparents.

Before Daria could exit Nina's room, Sydney, her seven-year-old 'going on 70', entered clumsily and, rubbing her eyes, no doubt abruptly awakened by laughter coming from her big sister's room.

"What's all the laughing about?" she asked in her ever so inquisitive tone.

Sydney was Daria's little masterpiece, and although she resembled her mother, her mannerisms were much like Auntie Tasha's. It was comical to witness. Sydney was the creative yet funny one in the family, with her sharp wit and overexaggerated vocabulary. At only seven years old, she was a whole vibe. Her inquisitiveness, boldness, vision, and sense of humor were all packaged into this fiery ball of energy. "Tasha's mini-me," Daria thought.

"Get dressed, Syd! We are going to Virginia with Auntie Tasha," Nina blurted out.

"Yes, Syd, go get dressed and pack your bag. You guys will be hanging out with Auntie Tasha and your grandparents for a couple of weeks."

"Why, Mommy?"

"Stop asking so many questions," her big sister scolded. Nina often liked being the oldest sibling because she found pleasure in being the authoritarian.

"Nina!" Daria gave a scolding glance before turning her attention back to little Sydney. "It is because they miss you and want to spend time with you."

Daria enjoyed the interaction between her two daughters most days. Still, she sometimes worried about Nina taking her big sister role a little too far. She appreciated her boldness but did not want to nurture a bully. They embodied such different personalities, yet one could not survive without the other. Nina was clearly the voice of authority, while Sydney enjoyed submitting to her big sister. Mostly because Nina often enjoyed playing teacher with Sydney, and Sydney enjoyed art or music time in their makeshift classroom. Sydney ran into her room to pick out an outfit and then back into Nina's room to get dressed. As the girls gathered their things,

Daria went to the nursery, which had been converted into a toddler room. Her one and only son, Isaiah, was playing with one of his favorite toys while lying in his big boy bed. Time had flown since they first moved to Charlotte. She smiled at her son, almost three years old, who would celebrate a birthday in a few weeks. They should be planning a birthday party, not worried about his father sitting in the back of a police car.

"Hey, little man," Daria said as she entered his room.

"Hi, Mommy!" his little voice rang out in glee.

"It's time to get dressed. You and your sisters are going on a trip with Auntie Tasha."

"Tee Tee, Tasha?" he repeated excitedly.

"Yes, so let's get moving as fast as we can." Daria found it easier with Isaiah if she turned everything into a game. This morning's game was how quickly could he get dressed. She grabbed a cute little outfit from his closet, and in record time, he had his shirt on backwards and his pants to his ankles. Yet he proudly shouted, "I win," as he raised his arms in what he thought was his victory. Daria could not help but laugh as she saw her son's attempt at dressing himself. His tiny frame was hidden under his oversized shirt. She took a few moments to put his shirt on correctly and pull up his little pants. His cute round face beamed with pride. "Yes, you won." She quickly packed his suitcase and sent Isaiah to play school with his sisters until Tasha arrived.

Realizing she had already planned their trip without consulting with Tasha, she rushed to her bedroom to grab the phone and call her dearest friend and lifeline. Tasha was in town conducting business for their restaurant, Taste of Heaven. She often came to town for business but always padded her trips with extra time to visit with her best friend as often as possible. Daria knew, particularly given the current circumstances, Tasha would quickly step in to do what was needed. Daria knew Tasha was scheduled to leave in a few days. She was grateful her friend did not hesitate to change her plans. She also called Sister Treva, their trusted prayer warrior and good friend of the family.

Tasha immediately agreed to take the kids to Daria's parents while Daria and Devon waded through this apparent misunderstanding. She wasted no time pulling her belongings together and jumping in the shower after the call. They all hoped it was a simple misunderstanding and Devon would return home soon. Even so, this would give Devon and Daria some alone time for a week or two. With everything Tasha and Daria had been through in the past, there would be no way Tasha would not come to her friend's side in her time of need.

Her hotel was fifteen minutes from Daria's home and what Tasha liked to call the 'Royce Estate.' She knew they had plenty of room, and she could have easily stayed in her home, but Tasha always respected her friend's marriage. Although she would never cross any lines with Devon, she wanted to avoid all opportunities for people to spread negativity.

"Daria, are you okay?" Tasha burst through the door of the Royce Estate.

Without a word, Daria embraced her friend. She was a ball of self-contained emotions until she saw the face of her lifelong friend. Once they hugged, there was no turning back, and emotions instantly seeped out. Surprisingly, it was the release Daria needed to remove the weight she carried while strengthening herself for Devon and the children.

"Honestly, Tasha, I don't know if I am or not. This is crazy! Why would the police come to question Devon? I just don't understand."

That makes two of us, Sis, but we will get to the bottom of it. In the meantime, I will take my beautiful nieces and nephew home to your parents, so you have one less thing to worry about."

"Thank you again. I'm sorry for cutting your trip short."

"Don't you say another word. Never apologize for needing me, Sis! We have always and will always be there for each other."

"Absolutely!" Daria agreed. The kids are upstairs in their rooms. After getting them dressed, I told them they could play until Auntie Tasha arrived. They are always so excited to spend time with you."

"I feel the same about them."

"They haven't eaten breakfast yet...."

"Don't worry about it; you know I will take good care of my babies. I will stop along the way and get something to eat, and I will spend time with them once we make it back to Virginia. I will take them to your parents later this evening."

"You are the absolute best! My parents are already expecting them. They know how 'Tee-Tee Tasha' is, so it is safe to say they will not be looking for any of you anytime soon," both ladies laughed.

Before they could say anything else, the doorbell rang. Tasha went upstairs to get the children while Daria answered the door. It was Sister Treva dressed in a red graphic tee with white lettering which read 'Prayer Soaked.' The words were accented with what looked like splashes of water. She matched it with a beautiful red, white, and black maxi skirt. Daria stepped aside to let Sister Treva enter.

"Thank you for coming on such short notice, Sister Treva," she began as she hugged her friend.

"Anything for you, baby. So do we know any details at this point?"

"No, nothing yet. Tasha is upstairs getting the kids ready for their trip. Do you mind accompanying me to the police station? I need your strength and your prayers. I know you will be able to 'pray me calm.' My emotions can sometimes preclude my judgment. I need at least one of my rocks by my side. I wish you could both come with me, but it makes more sense for the kids to stay with Mom and Dad until we figure this out. I am just grateful Tasha was already in town for business."

Soon after, Tasha descended the stairs. She looked like the Pied Piper with Isaiah in her arms while Sydney and Nina were riding her heels. Daria loved how much her children loved Tasha and how much she loved them. Because of medical complications in her past, Tasha could no longer have children of her own, which hurt her deeply. Still, being such a strong person, she bounced back quickly. Or maybe Tasha buried her feelings well enough to seem as though she bounced back. Either way, she was thrilled when Daria and Devon had children. She always said they had three because one was for her, making it all the more comical that Sydney acts just like her.

"Well, hello, Sister Treva!" Tasha exclaimed in her own sassy 'Tasha' way, "Ma'am, don't hurt 'em with this ensemble."

"Get over here, silly lady, and give me a hug," Sister Treva grinned, embracing Tasha.

She always seemed to have an affinity for Tasha. Maybe because Sister Treva could not have children of her own, she, too, could relate to Tasha's struggle. They both desired to have children, but God saw a different path for them. Even though it was not what either originally wanted, God filled the void with people and purpose.

"Oh wait, now...what does that say? 'Prayer Soaked'...you betta rock wit it! Honey, the glow-up is real!"

"Only you, Tasha, only you!"

Daria chimed in as they all laughed heartily. Even little Isaiah giggled though he had no idea what was funny.

"What? Sister Treva knows how I am. We cool like that," she said as she winked at Sister Treva. "Seriously, ladies, please keep me posted on what is happening and let me know if you need me to head back this way. Being the boss has its privileges," Tasha hugged her friend and gave Sister Treva a kiss on the cheek before she headed to her car with the children in tow.

"Will do, Tasha! Thank you again for doing this for me. We are right behind you."

"Yes, let's get there so Pastor Devon can feel our presence. I sense the beginning of a storm brewing. He is going to need us all to keep him soaked in prayer," responded a clever Sister Treva.

Chapter 3

$\mathcal{D}$aria and Sister Treva sat in the crowded police station for a few hours before laying eyes on Devon. Sister Treva was a welcome distraction for Daria as the ladies prayed, not just for Devon but for everyone who shared the police lobby with them. They knew when trouble came a calling, it was always best to be about God's business until He calmed the storm. After extensive prayers, they chatted the remaining time away. Sister Treva understood her assignment, and even though her Spirit strongly suggested trouble brewing, she wanted to keep Daria as calm as possible.

"Lady Daria," Sister Treva interrupted the silence, "Do you have any idea why the police brought Pastor Devon here?"

"Sister Treva, I don't. I mean, they were asking if he knew someone named Jocelyn. Then they began asking where he was last night. It was strange. Except for running out to the church yesterday evening, he was with the kids and me all day."

"No matter, honey, and don't you fret. It sounds like the police are just asking Devon questions. They're guessing some crime was committed, and they want to ask the good Pastor a few questions to help them capture the suspect. You know Pastor Devon has a lot of connections — maybe he just holds the answer to their missing puzzle piece."

"I really hope you are right, Sister Treva."

****

Johnston opened the door to the small interrogation room and made a motion with his hands indicating Devon was free to leave.

Devon shook his head as he stood up and said to Johnston, "None of this makes sense."

He walked out of the interrogation room into the hallway. The cramped musty room took a toll on him, and he was able to breathe better. Devon followed a uniformed police detective who was standing just outside the door. He was escorted back into the main lobby of the police station. When Daria saw her husband appear in the doorway, she quickly jumped to meet him. She ran into the peace she could only find in her husband's arms. They embraced for a long moment. When she pulled away, tears streamed down her face.

"Are you okay?" Daria asked, concerned and inspecting her husband to ensure he had no scars or bruises.

"Yes baby, I am okay," Devon replied as he lovingly wiped the tears from her eyes.

"What is this about?" she asked almost before Devon could complete his response to her initial question.

"Baby, can we get out of here? I will try to explain everything when we get home."

"Yes, of course," she agreed as she looked around the room. The reality of where they were sat in once again.

Daria turned to Sister Treva, the mightiest prayer warrior they had ever encountered. "Thank you so much for being here with me," she gratefully embraced Sister Treva. "I don't know how I could have dealt with any of this if you hadn't been by my side."

"No worries at all. We are family; I would not dare let you enter this fight alone. This isn't just an attack in the natural," Sister Treva answered.

"Ah, Sister Treva, thank you so much for sitting with my wife. You two must have been here for hours," Devon responded as he hugged her for her commitment to his family.

"Only three and a half hours or so, yet it was but a blink of an eye in God's sight."

"I wish I had God's sight because I felt every bit of the three and a half hours," Devon tried to crack a little smile to lighten the intensity of his current situation. "If it is not too much of an imposition, once we get home, would you mind coming in as well, Sister Treva? We could really use our strongest prayer warrior by our side."

"Of course, Pastor."

On the drive home, the trio was quiet. Daria could tell Devon was having a serious conversation with the Lord, so she dared not interrupt them. This had always been his process when dealing with his most intent struggles. It helped him digest whatever struggle consumed him. She likened it to the encounter with Jacob as he wrestled with the angel and declared he would not let go until he received his blessing. She knew he would share what happened once they were home. God never failed them, and she knew He would honor His promises, even in this storm. When they arrived home, the trio made their way up the driveway and into the house. Daria went into the kitchen to get them all something to drink. She placed a stunning serving tray on the coffee table containing a cold pitcher of lemonade and three glasses of ice. As if on autopilot, she poured each of them a cold glass before the conversation began. Daria was always the supreme host. She went out of her way to make sure everyone felt welcomed in her home. Once they all settled themselves in the living room, Pastor Devon prepared himself to speak.

Sister Treva would not dare claim she knew Pastor Devon as well as his beloved wife, but she did know his tells when he was heavily burdened. She saw the frown lines on his forehead and watched as he wrestled with finding the right words to say. She sat silently, sipping her lemonade while he processed his thoughts. She knew God would give him the right words.

"Ladies," Devon began after he downed almost half his glass of lemonade. Daria and Sister Treva diverted their attention to him with respectful gazes. "This is a lot, so before you interrupt or ask questions, let me get everything out."

"Of course," they responded as an echo of one another.

Once Devon completed sharing what happened in the interrogation room, the ladies sat stunned. They were clearly trying to wrap their heads around what Devon had just shared. Both understood the severity of the situation and wanted to fully comprehend the information before responding.

Daria broke the silence, "This is absurd! How could they possibly think you are capable of murder? And who is this eyewitness?"

"I don't know, baby; I am just as baffled as you are."

"We need to call Attorney Harris to get to the bottom of this!" Daria insisted.

"I think that's a good idea. Please schedule a meeting with Rich as soon as possible. They did not arrest me but warned me not to leave the city."

Attorney Richard Harris was a good friend and an incredible attorney. He had been a faithful member of Faith Hope and Love Church since before Devon had stepped in as pastor. Rich, as he was affectionately known, offered his services to the church at a discounted fee but insisted his services were pro bono for Pastor Devon. Rich assured Pastor if there was ever a need, he would be there for him.

Devon looked over at Sister Treva as her silence caught his attention. Once he saw her posture, he instantly knew she was warring in the spirit for him. She sat with her elbows resting on her lap and her hands clasped with her fingers interlocked. Her eyes were closed, and she was rocking back and forth. He dared not interrupt because he needed all the prayers and warriors he could get.

Sister Treva Gordan was a faithful member of the church. She was retired, so her time was totally devoted to the work of the Lord. Her husband, John Gordon, who had also been a faithful member, passed away a few years before Devon and Daria arrived. JG, as many affectionately called him, had a heart attack at age fifty-two. It always amazed Devon how Sister Treva remained faithful to God even in the face of losing her husband and being told she was barren. It was as if her adversity drew her closer to the Master where most would have blamed God. Even in her worst moments, she saw the value in trusting God. Ah, if others could come to the same reality. 'I would rather live my hardest days with God than live superficially happy without Him,' Devon concluded. Although he and Daria never had the privilege of knowing JG, they knew he had to be a mighty man of God if he were married to Sister Treva. Devon had known many prayer warriors in his time, and he was known to belt out powerful prayers of his own, but he had never met anyone quite like Sister Treva. She reminded him of a female version of the Apostle Paul in the Bible. He had no doubt Sister Treva could match Apostle Paul's energy any day and maybe even exceed it. He often wondered if she mirrored Paul's intensity before she gave her life to God, like before Saul was converted to Paul. Still, he never broached the subject with her.

Once Sister Treva concluded her prayer, she reached over to touch Devon and Daria's hands. "I know this does not look good with the natural eye, but believe you me, God is up to something. The truth will be exposed."

With that, she got up, grabbed her purse, and excused herself. Daria walked her to the door. Sister Treva turned to Daria and gave her a reassuring glance as she spoke. "Don't you worry your pretty little head over this. God said there is an evil force at work here, but rest assured, its deception will be exposed."

"Thank you, Sister Treva," Daria hugged her once again before she left.

"Dee?" As he affectionately often referred to Daria.

"Yes baby, what is it?" she responded.

"Please tell me you don't believe I could have anything to do with a, with a...," he stumbled over the words, "a murder."

"Of course not! The man I love could never kill another person. Your mission is to bring faith, hope, and love. You don't have it in you to do such a thing. Don't

43

worry about me, baby. My vows are true to this day; I will stand by you in good times and bad."

"Well, this is definitely bad if ever I saw it," Devon responded, embracing his wife. Every day, a different reason to love her was uncovered. With all the wrong things he'd done, marrying Daria was the best decision he could have ever made. Devon wished he could stand there and hold his wife forever, but he still had work to do before they had peace again.

It was as if Daria read his mind when she pulled away and looked up at her husband, "I guess we need to get ahead of this before the gossip mongers start to spew venom throughout the church. A lie in the wrong hands would be disastrous."

He was amazed at her discernment. Daria was gifted to know her husband's needs before he could verbalize them. This woman was indeed his help meet in every sense of the word and did not hesitate to move proactively. She always told him she would rather look a horse in its face than get kicked blindly standing behind it. Devon knew she was already thinking of the blowback this would have on the church and her family. He hated to see his wife worry. This was his burden to bear; he knew it would affect her and his family but would not allow it to burden her any more than necessary.

"Dee, I will call Deacon Maurice. He needs to hear this from me. I don't want you to worry about things at the church. I promise you I will get to the bottom of this. My vows to you are still true as well. Baby, I promised to love, honor, and protect you. I pray you don't look upon me as a failure." Devon hung his head at the very thought of letting down his beloved.

Daria listened intently as her husband spoke, but she responded as soon as she had an opening. "Devon, you did not commit this crime; therefore, I could never look at you as a failure. You are my lifeline, and I am yours. I know you are a good man, and the people of the church know it, too. If some choose to walk away, so be it. We didn't need them in our camp to begin with. You know God has a way of separating the wheat from the tare. We will get through this, but it will only happen if we do it together."

"You're right. Thank you for the reminder. I love how you hold me up when I'm weak. You are an amazing woman," he leaned in to give her a passionate kiss.

"Ok, so let's get back to business," Daria responded, blushing from the kiss. "I will schedule an appointment with Attorney Harris as soon as possible."

"Thank you! I am glad you are on my side. Thanks for calling Tasha to pick up the kids. I don't know what I would have done if they saw the police take me away."

"I agree; I think we wore them out with Carowinds yesterday, so they slept in. When they woke up, I told them you were handling some business and would be back as soon as you could. I asked my parents if Tasha could bring the kids to them. They are elated to spend quality time with their grandkids, but of course, they are so worried about you. They send you their love and their prayers. Plus, I couldn't imagine you at the police station without me. I figured we may need them out of the house until we could get to the bottom of this nightmare."

"Thank you, baby! I knew you would ride with me through any storm from the moment I met you."

Daria glanced back at Devon and blew him the cutest Betty Boop kiss as she left to make her phone call and start lunch. It was already one o'clock, and neither of them had eaten...how could they? But she knew they would need all their physical and spiritual strength to fight the war that lay ahead for them.

Chapter 4

*D*evon left the dining room and headed to his place of refuge, which held most of his deepest secrets. The cozy study, with its charcoal gray walls accented with two adjacent light gray walls trimmed in white, was the perfect place to unwind. Feeling a bit out of sorts, Devon sat in his executive chair to decompress and avoid falling from the day's overwhelming, dizzying thoughts. He shuffled papers on the massive mahogany desk. His thoughts were too deep to concentrate, so he moved to his black leather couch across from his desk. His mind was on the accusation—the elephant in the room. God, how are you going to get the glory from this? He understood how God allowed things to befall His children because He knew they would remain faithful. God had to have a greater plan than to see him in prison. Particularly over a murder he did not commit. He searched the room for something, anything to distract him. His eyes landed on a picture hanging on the adjacent wall; it was of him and Daria. It instantly made him smile. How did he become so blessed? He closed his eyes and allowed his mind to reminisce on their beginnings.

****

To Devon, Daria Hendrix-Royce was the most beautiful woman in the world. She was co-owner of a very successful restaurant, Taste of Heaven, in their former town of Smithfield, North Carolina. She and her best friend, Tasha Barron, opened the restaurant together shortly after graduating from Norfolk State University. Daria had not had an easy life, but she made the best out of even her worst days. She often said her testimony was," Thank God I do not look like what I have been through." She was a survivor of sexual assault and domestic violence and had a story to tell.

Not far from Taste of Heaven was a small church, Grace Temple. Several of the congregants from the church often visited her restaurant. Daria overheard conversations about how God's anointing always resided in this little church and knew she needed to be part of a local body of believers. With all she had gone through in her life, she especially knew God was a healer and deliverer. Daria attended their Bible study classes on Wednesday evenings and church services on Sundays when she had enough help in the restaurant to cover. Her partner and best friend, Tasha, was a marketing genius but did not spend much time at the restaurant. Tasha took her career seriously. She was always networking with clients, connecting with new vendors, and building relationships to help the restaurant grow. On the other hand, Daria loved coming into the restaurant every day. She still enjoyed cooking in the beautiful kitchen and mingling with her employees and customers.

One evening, Pastor Jonathan Royce and his favored son Devon Royce came in for dinner. Of course, she recognized them immediately and came out to greet them. They welcomed her to join them so they could learn more about her. She had shared parts of her past with them during the various Bible study sessions. She found their Bible studies were not just about learning the Bible but also learning the character of those they serve within the church.

"Sister Daria, I am fascinated with your story of tragedy to triumph," Pastor Royce said as he recalled bits of her testimony.

"Thank you, sir. I don't know what I would have done if God hadn't been with me," she thoughtfully responded. Daria was always happy to share her testimony. Even through her trials, the story of how she navigated her youth 'shedding silent tears' was all to glorify God. The two men were amazed by her transparency and asked if ministering to other women by sharing her journey was ever a consideration. Daria said she would think about it but had a little hesitancy. It was one thing to talk about what happened to her, but it was something else entirely to minister to others. Ministry meant being responsible for others' souls. She did not esteem herself as worthy of such an important assignment. She thanked the gentlemen for allowing her to spend time with them. As the server came with their meal, she exited so the men could peacefully enjoy their food.

Before departing, Daria told the server their meal was on her. She smiled, made her way across the dining area, and disappeared behind the swinging doors to the far back of the restaurant. The kitchen and the offices were beyond this door. As Daria headed towards her office, she was greeted by Tasha, her business partner, who saw her conversing with Pastor Royce and his son. She grabbed her by her arm and whisked her away into the office.

"Since when did you start dining with the guests, ma'am?" Tasha teased.

"Why are you always so nosey?" Daria retorted.

"You know you need me to look out for you. But seriously, wasn't that Pastor Royce and his son?" Tasha inquired.

"Yes, they came from a leadership meeting and decided to stop for dinner before going home."

"Mr. Royce, Jr is cute!" Tasha smiled as she looked through a one-way window in the office.

"I guess he's alright," Daria said as she pretended to busy herself with restaurant business.

"Oh, so that's how you feel?"

"I don't have time to entertain your foolishness. I know where this conversation is going. I love you, sis, but you know how my track record has been with men."

"None of us have always made the right choices, but you shouldn't give up on dating."

"I didn't say I gave up. And how do you know if the guy is even interested?"

"Mama knows..." Tasha teased as she sassed out of the office.

The following Sunday, Daria, and Tasha attended services at Grace Temple. Pastor Royce had been grooming Devon to someday lead his own church, so on this Sunday, Devon rose to preach. Tasha poked Daria in the leg as he made his way to the podium. The duo had no idea he would be preaching. Pleasantly surprised, the pair looked at each other and smiled.

After service, Devon stood at the door greeting people as they exited the church. Tasha and Daria approached him.

"Hello, ladies. I am glad you could join us today," Devon began.

"Thank you," Tasha responded, "your sermon was very inspiring."

"Praise God," Devon continued, "I am so glad you enjoyed it."

"My friend Daria enjoyed it as well. You remember Daria, right? By the way, what is your official title? I don't want to be disrespectful."

"Tasha!" Daria gave her friend a warning glance.

Tasha shrugged her shoulders. "I'm just trying to be in order in the house of the Lord."

"When are you ever in order?" Daria laughed.

"You ladies are funny. How could I forget the lovely Daria Hendrix? Please call me Devon. My title here is Assistant Pastor, but I don't get hung up in all that stuff."

"Daria," Devon held out his hand to embrace hers. "I am happy to see you are still visiting with us. Maybe someday soon, you will take the leap of faith and join our humble piece of heaven on earth."

"You never know," Daria blushed. She really had been considering membership but now felt it would be awkward. She did not want Devon to think she only joined the church because of a possible attraction.

About a month later, Daria found herself leaving her seat and approaching the front of the church during alter call. The Spirit of the Lord was so powerful; it was as if God Himself lifted her from her seat. She decided it was time to commit to Grace Temple Church since attending Bible Study and Sunday service was more regular and enjoyable. What was stopping her? She could do nothing but comply with how God moved in this service. God picked her up and floated her to the front of the church before she realized it. Tasha was elated to see her friend move in this direction. Although the traditional church was not her scene, she knew this was just what Daria needed.

Shortly after becoming a member, Daria started attending the Women's Ministry meetings, where she found some amazing ladies who had awesome testimonies about the goodness of God. She really felt a connection with these women. Most were around her age, but a few were a little older. It was a nice mix of youth and wisdom. Everyone seemed to genuinely love and respect each other. The ministry was led by the First Lady of the church, Mrs. Royce, Pastor Royce's wife. Or as she liked to tease, the One and Only Lady of the church. Mrs. Royce was extremely anointed. The glow of the shekinah glory of God was all over her. She was wise yet humble, easy to talk to, and so down to earth. She exuded a level of kindness and love Daria had never experienced before.

A few months after she joined the church, First Lady Royce asked for a meeting with Daria. The two ladies met at Taste of Heaven for tea.

"Daria," Lady Royce began, "I am so intrigued by you and your story."

"Thank you," Daria responded.

"I have two asks of you."

"Sure."

"I would love for you to consider being one of our speakers for our young adult conference. It is three months away, but I am a stickler for planning and preparation. You don't have to give a sermon or anything like that. We find it more effective to have our younger adults mentor one another. Therefore, this would be more of a 'TED Talk,' if you will. You don't even have to give details about your past if you aren't comfortable. Maybe share about being a lady entrepreneur...better yet, just speak whatever God puts on your heart."

"Wow, Lady Royce! I don't know what to say." Daria responded.

"Just say you will do it." Lady Royce teased.

"I would be delighted."

"I am so happy to hear that."

"But wait, what's the other ask?"

"Our church members always rave about this restaurant of yours. Would you also consider having your staff cater the event? Of course, we would compensate accordingly."

"Really? It would be my honor."

"Wonderful! My son, Devon, is over the conference, so you can work with him on the logistics."

Daria's eyes lit up at the thought of working with Devon. Lady Royce saw the spark but did not say anything. She had discerned a connection between Devon and Daria but did not want to intervene. She knew God would make the divine connection if it was His will. The ladies spent another hour chatting over tea and getting to know each other. Lady Royce glanced at her watch.

"Oh my! Where did the time go?"

"Goodness, I hope I am not keeping you from anything Lady Royce."

"Not at all, dear. I just want to get home before Pastor Royce. I like to have his slippers and hot tea by his favorite chair when he gets home. I always try to set a pleasant atmosphere for my husband to come home to. An atmosphere that would make him not want to leave. I usually have jazz music playing low in the background because I know it relaxes him, and I burn his favorite sandalwood oil blend."

"Oh wow! I could really learn a lot from you about being a good wife!"

"Oh, are you about to cross the marital threshold?"

"No, ma'am. I'm not even dating anyone presently, but it never hurts to prepare until he comes."

"Indeed, it doesn't," Lady Royce winked at Daria as she got up to leave.

The ladies hugged as they parted ways. This was only the beginning of Daria working in various capacities at Grace Temple. She and Devon began spending more time together in ministry. They found they had quite a bit in common and enjoyed being in each other's presence. Whenever they had a meeting, Devon always started and ended the meeting in prayer. Daria could see how much he loved God. But what she could not see was the love spark that was igniting between the two of them.

Daria was finishing her notes after one of the bi-weekly Young Adult Ministry Meetings. Everyone else was packing belongings, chatting, and leaving the fellowship hall. Devon sat at a table diagonal to hers, also finishing his final thoughts. As he looked up to say goodbye to one of the church members sitting across from him, Daria caught his eye. He marveled at how intently she worked. She came into the ministry with such tenacity, unlike a few other members who joined just to make friends and possibly a love connection. This was nothing new within young adult ministries. But he could tell she was not here to play games. She was on assignment. It almost reminded him of the character of Ruth and how she was busy tending to work when Boaz noticed something different about her compared to other women in the field. Just as Boaz was compelled to take care of Ruth, Devon felt similarly towards Daria. He decided to ask her to dinner, but he was so engrossed in his thoughts he did not notice her gathering her things. As she stood up to leave, he immediately left his seat so as not to miss an opportunity to speak with her.

"Daria," he said to get her attention.

"Hey Devon, what's up?" she replied.

"Do you have any plans tomorrow evening?"

She thought for a moment before she responded. "Nothing at the moment. My business partner is at the restaurant this week, which freed up my evenings. Is there something you need me to do for the church?"

He smiled at her response and genuinely sensed she was mission-minded. He was impressed by this and by her.

"No, no...it's not church-related," he said as he cleared his throat. "Would you like to have dinner with me tomorrow night?"

"Dinner?" Daria said with a hint of surprise in her voice.

"Yes, dinner, you do eat, don't you?" he laughed as he commented.

"So, you have jokes? Yes, I eat. I own a whole restaurant, remember? I just didn't expect you to ask me out."

"Oh really, so that tells me you at least thought about it."

"Don't flatter yourself," she laughed.

"Well...what do you think? Would you like to have dinner with me tomorrow night?"

Daria paused before giving an answer. Her initial response was to politely decline, but then she heard Tasha's voice in her head. "You haven't really dated anyone in some time. He is handsome, and if he asks you out, you should go out!"

"Sure," she shyly responded, giggling at the thought of her best friend.

"Awesome...then it's a date. I've wanted to try the new restaurant and jazz spot over on Central Avenue."

"A jazz spot? I didn't take you for the jazz type."

"Really? What did you take me for?"

"I hadn't really thought about it."

"Ahhh, that hurt," Devon replied as he pretended to pull a dagger out of his heart.

"More jokes," she laughed.

"I won't keep you any longer. I can come by and pick you up around 7 p.m. tomorrow?"

"Yes, 7 p.m. works for me."

Daria grabbed the last of her things as she headed for the door. She looked back at Devon, who smiled as she walked away. She returned his smile and gracefully exited the building.

On her drive home, she thought about the cute little exchange between her and Devon. She promised herself a long time ago she would not lose herself in a man again. She had no expectations about this date. In her mind, it was two friends having dinner. She decided not to share this bit of information with her best friend. She knew Tasha would go overboard if she knew about the date. When it came to Daria and relationships, her intentions were pure. But she liked to put Daria on the fast track when most times, Daria wanted to take things nice and slow.

Chapter 5

*D*aria scheduled a meeting with Attorney Harris later in the afternoon. As requested by her husband, they planned a meetup at the church, which included Deacon Maurice, Sister Treva, his dear friend Joshua Evans and his wife, Stephanie. After seeking the Lord, Devon clearly heard these people would remain faithful through this life-altering storm. Some would stay, others would distance themselves, but these were those who the Lord ordained to be a part of his inner circle. He needed them to hear the accusations and to keep him girded up with prayer. After hearing everything, Pastor Devon's office erupted with many questions and verbal expressions of disbelief. After a few minutes, Attorney Harris stood up, and the room grew silent.

"When Lady Daria reached out and told me what happened, I immediately made some calls. I reached out to my contacts to find out what the police knew and the level of involvement they think Pastor Devon has in this. We all know Pastor Devon had nothing to do with murdering this young woman, but I needed to find out what they know."

"And...what do they know?" asked Joshua.

"Apparently, they have eyewitnesses who put Pastor Devon at the crime scene. Not just places him there, but they say they witnessed the beating of this young lady."

"That's preposterous! Unbelievable! Who are these eyewitnesses?" Joshua retorted.

"I don't have names yet, but I am working on it," he turned to acknowledge Joshua and his frustration. "I also found out they have skin and blood samples they are running forensic tests on."

"Good, that should prove my innocence," Devon chimed in.

"Yes, I agree. But we must be cautious from here on out. It clearly appears to be a setup of sorts, but they seem pretty sure of themselves. I would advise you all to stay vigilant. Someone is out to get the good Pastor, so we don't want to give them any ammunition to use."

"What do you mean? Do you think they will tamper with the DNA evidence?" Daria asked with a worried look on her face.

"It's not likely but also not out of the realm of possibility," Attorney Harris responded. Look, I don't want any of you to get any more upset than you already are. Most Detectives are decent enough, but until we can get some answers, I would prefer we stay ready so we don't have to get ready. Pastor Devon, please be extra careful in what you do, what you say, and how you conduct yourself from here on out. Make sure someone is with you at all times. I know it's not an easy task with your busy schedule, but you need to be sure you have someone who can testify to your every move from this point forward."

"I can take care of that," Joshua insisted.

"This is ridiculous!" Devon exclaimed. "Now I need a babysitter?"

"Baby, if Attorney Harris thinks that's best, then that's what we will do," responded Daria. "I can be with you during the day while you run errands. Sister Treva, Deacon Maurice, and Sister Angelique can account for your whereabouts while you are at church or ministry runs."

"And I can handle the night shift," an eager Joshua chimed in. "You know I am retired military, and I have been telling you for months now you need to be guarded. Not that you are a haughty preacher, but I have been sensing in my gut something was about to happen. I have shared this with you and with my wife."

"Yes, Josh has been increasingly worried about you over the last few months, Pastor. He has had these dreams. You were under attack, and no one was around to help you," Stephanie said, breaking her silence.

"All of this sounds good," Attorney Harris replied as he grabbed his briefcase. He placed a hand on Pastor Devon's shoulder and whispered in his ear, "God's got you, and so do we."

"Hang on a minute. Before anyone leaves this room, we need to pray," Sister Treva insisted as she stood up, reaching for the hands of Lady Daria to the left of her and Pastor Devon to the right. Everyone followed suit, grabbing the person's hands to their left and right. Sister Treva prayed a powerful prayer of covering and protection over Pastor Devon and a prayer for peace and strength for the family of the young lady who lost her life. She even prayed for the person or people who may have committed this crime and those who were accusing Pastor Devon.

"Amen," everyone said in unison.

The crowd began to disperse, leaving only Sister Treva, Deacon Maurice, and Pastor Devon in the office. They stayed back to construct a plan to preemptively control the narrative before it spread like wildfire throughout the church. Daria needed to step out to call Tasha. She needed to know they were safe and catch Tasha up on what had transpired.

"Hey, sis," Tasha said in her usual gleeful tone.

"Hey girl, just checking in to make sure the kids are good."

"Of course. We made it to Virginia with no problem. Now, we're at the beach. After such a long drive, I thought they would appreciate stretching their legs and releasing some of that energy. Girl, these kids wore me out with all their exuberance."

"I know they can be a handful. Thank you for being you."

"You know I will do anything for you guys. So, any updates on Devon?"

"Yes, he wasn't arrested. At least not yet."

"Arrested! What on earth? Why would anyone think Devon was involved in anything illegal?"

"Your guess is as good as mine. Tash, it just doesn't make sense."

"What doesn't? What happened?"

Daria gave Tasha an abbreviated rundown of what they knew so far. The two held the phone in silence, as it was just as unbelievable for Tasha to hear it as it was for Daria to share. After a few moments, Tasha spoke up. "Sis, I know this is difficult, but remember who you married and, more importantly, who you both serve."

"I know, Tash, but murder?"

"You and I both know he isn't capable of murder. Do not allow yourself to spiral, Daria. You have come out of the fire of tribulation unscathed. We both have. Believe he will, too. God has to have a greater purpose in this test. He has a plan, just as He did for you and for me, sis."

"I know, and I appreciate you, sis. It's just I thought we were well past all the drama. This has blindsided all of us."

"In this world, you will have tribulation, but be of good cheer; God has overcome the world."

"Tash, there you go, randomly quoting the Bible as always. Somehow you know just what I need just when I need it!"

"You know me...I can still flex in the faith," Tasha laughed.

"Flex in the faith? That's the Tasha I know and love." Both ladies had another laugh at Tasha's wit. They talked for a few minutes longer. After exchanging 'I love you' sentiments, they ended their call.

A crucial church meeting was scheduled for Saturday. Angelique was asked to send out urgent emails and text blasts to all church members. They needed not to tarry as this was a dire matter which could ultimately divide the church if not handled carefully. It was already Friday evening. Devon thought, "Where had the day gone?" The house was quiet without the children. Daria retired upstairs after complaining of a terrible migraine headache. Devon was disheartened at the idea of causing his wife pain. He did not simply love his wife; he was in love with her and vowed to protect her at all costs. And now, who would protect her from what was about to befall him?

Devon quietly entered the bedroom where his beautiful wife lay sleeping. As he changed clothes and into his pajamas, he thanked God for allowing him to marry someone so beautiful, brave, and strong. If only they had known each other back when she was in high school and college. He wished he could take away all the pain she experienced. Yet, he knew her suffering brought her strength. Although it was difficult for her, God used the worst time in her life to mold her into the amazing wife who now lay before him. Devon kneeled by her side of the king-size bed and whispered a prayer of protection before retiring to his side. As he settled in, he pulled her close and held her until he fell asleep.

Everyone was already assembled at the church when Devon and Daria arrived. They could tell the word had spread like wildfire, and people were curious about what he would say. "We haven't had this level of attendance all year," Daria smiled, hoping to calm her husband's nerves as they graced the stage in front of the church. Deacon Maurice joined them as requested.

Without going into the details, the Pastor, Lady Daria, and Deacon Maurice shared with the congregation there was a spiritual attack targeting the pastor. His name was being tarnished, and it could even impact the church. The trio reassured everyone that any rumors they heard were inaccurate and they would all be resolved as soon as possible.

"I heard the Pastor got arrested," one busybody parishioner loudly spoke to her friend seated next to her.

"Just scandalous," shouted another.

"I heard he killed somebody," said yet another.

"Look," Pastor Devon chimed in. "Those of you who know me know...though I am not a perfect man...I would never commit the heinous act I have been accused of doing. If you would just stick with us and not let the enemy divide us, you will see we will come out victorious. God will get the victory, even in this."

"This just ain't right," Brother Lucas stood up as he addressed the congregation. "Ever since this pastor joined our church, I knew something wasn't right. I couldn't put my finger on it. Since his arrival, he's come in here changing things around...allowing things in the church that shouldn't be," He ranted while making overexaggerated gestures with his arms. "Now look!"

"Brother Lucas, that's not fair!" exclaimed Deacon Maurice. "Of course, this young preacher was going to come in and stir things up. It always happens whenever a baton is passed from one pastor to another. Their beliefs may be the same, but Pastor Devon brings youthfulness and vitality to our ministry that Pastor McIntyre admittedly did not have. Pastor McIntyre chose Pastor Devon because he had great ideas to bring in a fresh wave of new members while sustaining and appreciating the current members. These men talked extensively before a decision was made. I believe in the decisions of Pastor McIntyre because I know he is led by God, and I stand on that same premise with Pastor Devon."

"Thank you, Deacon Maurice!" Pastor Devon reached out to give him a brotherly embrace. Turning to Brother Lucas, "Now, I cannot make you stand with us, but I will ask you to do so. If you don't feel it is in you to stick with our ministry, then I cannot force you to stay. I just pray you would seek God before turning your backs on us."

"Maybe you should have sought after God before you put us in this position," an angry Brother Lucas exploded. "All ya can listen to these lies, but I...will not...be deceived!"

As Brother Lucas stood up to leave, several others abruptly followed. It was disheartening for Pastor Devon to watch the division in his congregation, primarily because of him.

Brother Lucas Jackson was a lifer at Faith Hope and Love Church with a flair for dramatics. He had been a member since he moved to the Charlotte area over twenty years ago, just months after the doors of the church had opened. He desired to someday be the lead deacon of the church, but he was passed up time and again. Deacon Maurice had been Pastor McIntyre's right-hand man for a long time. Pastor McIntyre trained Deacon Maurice up from the time he was a teenager. Brother Lucas knew there was little to no opportunity for promotion to the coveted position as long as Pastor McIntyre was over the church. But he thought the changing of the guards would be his opportunity to step up. Surely if Pastor McIntyre were retiring, Deacon

Maurice would follow. When Brother Lucas realized this would not happen, he used his office as a trustee to skew the books to make it look like Deacon Maurice was skimming from the church. Knowing it was wrong and even feeling terrible afterward, his fleshly desires overtook him. He did not expect Pastor Devon to bring in an accountant to review the books and ultimately find the discrepancy, which pointed right back to Brother Lucas.

Of course, he was reprimanded and stripped from his position as trustee. This caused even more anger and hurt to swell up in him. The shame kept him silent until this moment. He believed he now had adequate ammunition to cause a revolt in the church without having to devise underhanded schemes to make it happen. The Pastor himself caused this chaos, but Lucas thought he could use this opportunity to get what he always wanted. He thought he might reap the benefits if he spoke up and got some of the congregants on his side. This scandal far outweighed anything Devon had done in the past. Maybe the Pastor and Deacon Maurice would step down, and he could finally earn what he considered his rightful place.

Immediately after the church meeting, Deacon Maurice shared his concerns about Brother Lucas with Pastor Devon. "Pastor, his outburst today shows he is up to no good."

"I hear you, but I cannot believe Lucas hates me so much he would frame me for murder," Pastor Devon replied, shaking his head.

"I am not so sure I agree. Remember his past deeds, the scandal with the finances merely to frame me so he could sit me down? He showed us there was nothing he would not do to get what he wanted," Deacon Maurice reasoned. "At the very least, it is worth mentioning to Attorney Harris. He did say we need to be vigilant."

"I will not judge this man for what he has done in his past as I would not want anyone to judge me for my past sins. None of us would. I will share what transpired today with Rich, but I will not accuse the man of wrongdoing. Clearly, I know first-hand how that feels."

"It's going to be alright, Pastor. Over the past few years, we have weathered a few storms together. Surely, we will weather this one, too."

Chapter 6

"Lady Daria, how are you holding up?" Stephanie asked as they were leaving the church.

"Sis, I just don't know," Daria responded. "I mean, I know without a doubt Devon didn't do this, but who out there hates him enough to frame him for murder?"

"There are many sick people in this world. I know this will be sorted out."

"I wish I could be so sure. But I am extremely grateful for people like you and Josh, who have been by our side since we moved to Charlotte."

"Sis, it has been such a joy to have you and your family in our lives. I absolutely love the instant connection between Josh and Pastor Devon. When Josh was in his darkest moments, God brought Pastor Devon into his life. We are forever grateful."

"We all were what each other needed. Thank you, my beautiful sister. For the last few years, this church has been a blessing to us. Now we are looked upon by some as a curse."

"Not to those who matter. Do you want me to come over? I know Pastor and Josh needed to go out for a bit.

Since the kids are gone, I don't want you at the house alone. Especially now that word is getting out about what happened. Like I said before, there are some crazy people in the world."

"No, I think I will be okay."

"Maybe I posed that wrong. Are you going straight home because I am coming over," Stephanie said with a stern look on her face.

"I have a massage appointment now. I should be done in an hour."

"Then I will see you in an hour and thirty," both ladies laughed as they proceeded to their cars.

"Hello, Lady Daria. Would you like your usual thirty-minute massage?" The petite young lady at the desk asked as she stood to shake Daria's hand. Daria always appreciated the warm welcome she received anytime she visited the Tranquility Day Spa.

"I think I need a full hour today," Daria responded.

"Then a full hour it is. Your room is ready; select your essential oil fragrance of choice. There is already a robe and slippers in your room. Just open the door when you are ready for me to get started."

As Daria lay on the table, her masseuse put on a smooth, soft jazz tune as she serviced her client. She deliberately took time to ensure all the tension spots from Daria's back and shoulders were hit. After a bit of small talk, Daria closed her eyes and felt the tension slowly leaving her body. Her mind wandered to the day she and her family moved to Charlotte and Faith Hope and Love Church. She could not believe they had already celebrated their second Pastoral anniversary.

****

Faith Hope and Love Church was a small church with a modern architectural exterior. It had a big personality gauging from the front with its gold, red and black intermingled color siding. It was somewhat different from anything they had seen before. Still, it truly brought character and attention to the front of the church. On either side of the revolving door entryway were vast bay windows similar to those used for department store displays. There was a wooden cross tilted on its side and draped with a purple robe signifying the royalty of Jesus. The other window had an interesting depiction of Jesus ascending into heaven, which was backlit to illuminate His image. It was very detailed, even down to His nail-scarred hands. The lawn was freshly mowed, and various shrubs and flowers of all types and colors were meticulously landscaped throughout the grounds. The aromatic scents from the flower beds added to the charm.

As they walked through the revolving entryway, they entered the church lobby. On the wall to the left was a large television mounted on the wall displaying the church announcements. A small table underneath the television was neatly decorated with banners representing the ministry. It proudly displayed colorful pamphlets and postcards advertising the church and various activities. On the right of the entryway was an opening that led into the men's and women's restrooms. Each restroom had five stalls and three sinks. Upon entering the women's restroom, there was a little sitting area with a couch and a beautiful metal clock hung above it. A large metal vase with breathtaking floral displays subtly matching the clock was placed on both ends of the couch. Off the sitting room were the stalls with full-length mirrors on one wall. Another wall made of concrete blocks and painted a deep plum held the sinks, and the remaining walls were also concrete blocks and painted a neutral bone hue. Air hand dryers and optional paper towel dispensers hung along the walls, and several bins were strategically placed to dispose of discarded items. The women's restroom was quite dainty. The floral, herbal, evergreen scents of lavender and sweet vanilla fragrances greeted them from the wall-mounted air fresheners.

The men's restroom was nowhere near as inviting, but it was still quite attractive. The walls were the same texture and color as the women's restroom, except the purple accent wall was in front of the three urinals. There was no sitting area which made Devon chuckle. "Why would men want to sit around while other men used the urinal?" he thought. However, it was nice to smell a hint of sandalwood and amber permeating from the air fresheners.

A door in the Fellowship Hall led to the Pastor's office, and another led into the sanctuary. A banner on the back wall read, "Welcome, Pastor Devon and Lady Daria." On either side of the banner were several bouquets of balloons with each of the children's names, Nina, Sydney, and Isaiah, written in bold letters. Under the banner was a table elegantly set with assorted finger foods, fresh fruit, various cold juices, flavored waters, and soft drinks. "Wow," they said as they marveled at such a warm welcome. The church administrator, minister of music, and several others came out of the kitchen with a beautifully decorated cake.

"You guys didn't have to do all of this," Pastor Devon began as he took Isaiah out of his car seat so he, too, could enjoy the moment.

"Of course we did," responded one of the seasoned church ladies Pastor Devon recognized as Sister Treva Gordon. "We can't have our new first family move into town and not be greeted properly."

"Sister Treva, it is good seeing you again," he said as he walked over to give her a respectful hug.

"Not as good as it is to be seen," she laughed as she returned the hug. "Let me introduce you to Brother Joshua and Sister Stephanie Evans. I believe you have already met everyone else."

Pastor and Lady Daria exchanged pleasantries with the Evans and shared their excitement to get to know them. They learned Joshua was retired military. He served his country for ten years and was a decorated Detective. Stephanie was a physician assistant at Atrium

Hospital. They were an intriguing couple and one with which Daria hoped to become better acquainted.

"Daddy, I'm hungry," Sydney said as she tugged on her daddy's shirt, eyeing the table of goodies.

"After a five-hour car ride, I bet you all could stand to eat a little something," responded Angelique Dobson, the church administrator.

"We have a table prepared for you," added Maurice Duffy, the head deacon.

After the family shook hands and exchanged hugs, they were escorted to one of the beautifully decorated tables in the center of the fellowship hall. As they ate, they shared the adventures of their trip and their excitement to lead such a fantastic group of people. The girls ate, then left the table to admire their balloons and sneak another piece of cake. Isaiah had been passed over to Daria after she had finished eating so he could be fed. Though he could not eat table food, he was more than content with his baby food feast of pureed chicken and carrots.

"Lady Daria, your children are so beautiful and well-mannered," Angelique admired as she watched the young ladies play with their balloons.

"Thank you so much, Sister Angelique. At times they can be a handful, but overall, these three bring me so much joy." Daria responded.

Isaiah giggled an infectious baby laugh as he ate his food. Although he did not understand what was happening, the sweet toddler could sense the excitement and wanted to add his joyful noise to the mix.

"Pastor Devon, you must be proud of such a beautiful family," Deacon Maurice interjected. "We want you all to take your time to acclimate to the city and to enjoy each other. We won't bombard you with church business minutes after you've moved into town. How about we put some time on your books next week to share with you the lay of the land," asked Deacon Maurice. "We already have a team at your new house unloading your things, so all we want you and your family to do this weekend is relax."

"Pastor McIntyre wanted to be here to greet you and your beautiful family, but he was called away at the last minute. He will be preaching his final sermon this Sunday and passing the torch to you," added Sister Angelique.

"I don't know what to say," Daria began. "You guys truly thought of everything."

"Yes," Devon agreed in amazement.

"We absolutely adore Pastor McIntyre, but we know how much he desires to retire and hand the mantle to someone younger with a fresh vision and a powerful anointing. We all believe we have found those gifts in you," began Sister Treva. "God directed us to you, and I received confirmation from Him that you and your family will indeed take this ministry to levels we have yet to dream."

Devon did not know very much about Sister Treva, but one thing he could sense in the spirit was that she was a prayer warrior. Not just any prayer warrior, his spirit spoke that he needed her in his corner. She was his God-appointed prayer warrior. There was a sense of serenity he felt in her presence.

As Devon looked at his watch, he realized it was already a little past 3 p.m. He once again thanked his welcoming team for such a warm greeting. Daria and the girls helped to discard the plates and cups while Devon strapped little Isaiah back into his car seat.

"Thank you!" Daria, Nina, and Sydney waved as they finished cleaning and headed to the front door to meet Devon and Isaiah. Enthusiasm began to overtake them as they knew their next stop would be their new home. Devon and Daria had visited it before closing. They both agreed the home had character and charm. The Royces were not flashy people. They felt a modest home that was warm and inviting was better than a larger house with no character. The drive from the church to their new house took fifteen minutes, and they passed several restaurants, shopping centers, and a park along the way. Their SUV, a 2019 midnight blue Mazda CX-5, found its way into a freshly cemented driveway. The driveway led to the two-car garage of an attached beautiful brick two-story home with yellow accents. A glass storm door opened to a beautiful red front door. The contrast of colors was enchanting. Daria took a moment to marvel at the craftsmanship. Along the sidewalk leading to the front door were flower beds. Beautiful red, yellow, and white peonies mixed with low-growing sedums provided hardy green leaves. The most breathtaking multi-colored tulips swayed with the breeze in a smaller flowerbed along the front porch. Daria paused to look over at her husband. He knew tulips were her favorite flower, so she surmised he had something to do with them being there.

"What a beautiful home," Daria thought. She sensed the family would make many beautiful memories there.

****

"Lady Daria?" the masseuse whispered as she gently tapped Daria on her shoulder.

"Has it been an hour already?" Daria sat up, snatching herself back to the present.

"Yes, ma'am...a little over; I could tell you really needed to unwind."

"Indeed, I did! Thank you so much."

After Daria dressed, paid for her services, and left a generous tip, she headed home to meet Stephanie. As she turned onto her street, she noticed quite a bit of activity. More vehicles than usual were on their residential street. She saw neighbors out on their porches, in their doorways, or standing on their lawns, attempting to get a better look at the commotion. She slowly crept closer to her house and discovered a barrage of reporters lined up in front of her home. She stopped her car before being spotted and called Devon.

"Devon, there are so many people. I don't even know how I can get into the house. They have the driveway blocked."

"Where are you? Did they see you?"

"No, I am at the top of the street in front of the Cunningham's property."

"Stay there. Josh and I are close; we will be there in five minutes."

"Okay, I don't like this, Devon!"

"Neither do I, baby, but we will handle it together."

"Oh, Steph is supposed to meet me here. Let me call and warn her."

"Yes. You ladies stay put until Josh and I get there."

Daria remained in her car even after she saw Stephanie pull up behind her. She did not want to run the risk of being recognized. Several minutes later, Devon and Joshua pulled up and walked up to the crowd of reporters. Daria could see the heated exchange but could not hear what was said. Soon, Josh waved for her to pull up toward the driveway and into their garage. He waited for the door to close completely before opening the driver-side door to help her exit.

"Devon is in the house waiting on you. You two should pack a bag and come with Stephanie and me. We want to get you away from the madness, at least until everything calms down."

"Josh, I have to leave my home?" she asked while getting out of her car.

"I know it's not fair, but we must make your safety the top priority. I promise you it will not be long. We will get to the bottom of all this," Joshua reassured her.

"I know you will, and I appreciate you and Stephanie. Oh wait, Steph, she was right behind me."

"I told her to head home. We will take you to our house for now and then to a property we own not far from us but still off the radar."

"Thank you, Josh," she said as she entered her home.

"Baby, are you okay?" Devon asked as he greeted his wife at the door."

"Yes, I am okay, physically anyway."

"Dee...I cannot begin to tell you how sorry I am you have to go through this. It's not right. None of this is."

"You are correct, it's not right, but it's also not your fault. Let's get our things and get out of here. We are going to get through this together."

"I love you, Daria Hendrix-Royce."

"I love you more, Pastor Devon Royce."

Chapter 7

*W*hile Devon and Daria were inside getting their belongings, Joshua drove around to the back of the house. He surveilled the property and deduced the commotion was confined to the street in front of the house. Both Royce's cars were in the parking garage. Just as Devon and Joshua planned, Devon made sure to turn the light on in the bedroom and kitchen. Maybe the paparazzi outside their home would think they were still there while they escaped out the back door.

Before they could slip out the back, the doorbell rang.

"Don't answer that," Daria's voice was audibly shaken.

Joshua entered through the backdoor. "More bad news, man, the police are here."

"What?" Daria exclaimed.

"What now?" Devon whispered as he opened the front door.

Detectives Sneed and Johnston were on his front porch with several additional officers behind them.

"We have a warrant to search your home and church office."

"This is harassment!" Daria shrieked.

"It's ok, baby, let's let them do what they need to do. I am innocent. They will not find anything here or at the church."

Devon's phone rang. As he picked it up from the table, he saw it was Angelique. "Angelique, I already know. The police are there to search the premises."

"Pastor, how did you know?"

"They are here at my home as well. It's ok; assist them with anything they need. I don't have anything to hide."

Once Devon ended the call, with his hands raised, he slowly walked over to join Daria and Joshua in the living room. They all sat quietly, looking back and forth at one another and then at the officers making their way through every room of their home. Officer Johnston requested Devon provide them with the clothing and shoes he wore the night of the incident. After an extensive search, the police left Devon's home with those items and a gun case.

Once the door opened for the officers to exit the premises, the reporters met them with a barrage of questions. Cameras were flashing, and questions were flying. The officers held the reporters back as they made their way to their patrol cars. Devon quickly closed and locked the front door as he motioned for Joshua and Daria to go out the back.

"Joshua, let's drop Daria off with Steph while we go to the church," Devon insisted.

"But baby, are you sure that's a good idea," concern was written across Daria's face.

"Yes, they should be gone by the time we get there, but I want to find out what, if anything, they may have taken. I am also going to call Rich to see what he can find out."

As they drove up to the church, they met with an all too familiar scene. The parking lot and front lawn were swarming with reporters. Joshua instructed Devon to bend down out of sight as he drove past the reporters to the back parking lot. There was a back entrance not many people knew about. This was the best way for Devon to enter the church without the risk of being seen.

Devon had called Angelique on the drive to let her know they were coming. She met them at the back entrance. They thought it wise not to meet in his office.

"Angelique, what happened?" Devon asked.

"It was intense—they forced their way past me and went straight into your office after waving the warrant in my face. They asked me for the visitor's log and questioned me about the other night when Deacon Maurice and I called you to the church."

"What did you tell them?"

"Nothing really, they asked about someone named Jocelyn, but I don't know anyone with that name. They searched the log for her name but did not find it. The only person I met with that night was the poor lady who came in frantic and afraid. But her name was Trini."

"Did they take anything out of the office?" Joshua asked.

"They did have a bag, but I couldn't see what was in it. It was a small evidence bag, I guess. Pastor, they are trying to accuse you of murder. They mean business!"

"I know, but I can assure you both, I did not kill anyone," he turned his gaze from Angelique to Joshua to emphasize this point but more so to seek reassurance from them. He needed them to believe him.

Despite everything going on, Devon still had to preach in the morning. He grabbed his sermon notes from the office before he and Joshua left the church. Devon and Daria stayed at the Evans home for the night. Devon found that Joshua's mancave was ideal for tightening his notes. It was nothing like his study at home or the church office, but it was a quiet place for him to commune with God. After all the craziness, he had a lot to lay at His feet.

"God, what is going on? I don't understand any of this, and now my wife and children are affected by it. I know better than to ask 'why me.' But I must ask, when will this end? What did they find in the church office, and why did they take my gun and clothes? None of this makes sense to me."

Devon sat in silence for quite some time. Daria came to check on him, saw him kneeling by a desk chair, and knew he and God were in deep conversation. Wanting to ask him about what happened at the church, she decided it could wait and quietly shut the door to avoid interrupting her husband.

Sunday morning, Deacon Maurice called Josh when he got to church to notify him of the madness ensuing. He instructed Maurice to bring Pastor and Lady Daria around the back of the church to the basement door. Once they entered the basement, they were escorted to the Pastor's office. Devon and Daria peeked into the sanctuary anticipating a smaller attendance based on the responses from the church meeting the day before. However, what they saw was totally unexpected. To their surprise, there was a large crowd of people...standing room only. So many people, many of whom they knew, were either coming to get the latest gossip or be the ones to spread it. Included in the crowd were television and radio personalities, presumably the same groups that had encamped around their home. There was so much commotion one would have thought a celebrity was visiting.

"Have you seen Sister Angelique today?" Pastor Devon asked as he passed her empty office.

"No, I haven't seen her or heard from her. I am sure she is alright, probably shaken by this entire ordeal," Deacon Maurice assured him.

"You are probably right. This is crazy! How did we get here?"

"I don't know, Pastor, but I do know you need to show those people out there you are a confident man of God, and these lies have been formed straight from the pits of hell," Deacon Maurice asserted.

"You are right. I need to show them the power of God still resides in me, and I will boldly stand against the wiles of the devil. This is an opportunity to share God with people who may not know Him. I know the devil meant this as a setup. Still, with reporters and people from all over town here, this is my opportunity to witness and be a beacon of light even in my darkest hour. With the cameras rolling, imagine how many unsaved we could reach with God's Word. Our charge is to spread the gospel to all the land. Let's do it!"

"That's the Pastor I have grown to love," Deacon Maurice said as he patted Pastor Devon on the back. "If we continue to focus on you and this murder accusation, then God will not get the glory...let's turn this thing around!"

"Amen," Daria chimed in. "This is our opportunity to win souls or plant the seeds. Can you imagine the number of lives positively and forever altered by what the devil meant for evil? We are Faith Hope and Love Church, after all!"

The men agreed! "Where is Sister Treva?" Devon asked, noticing her absence. "I hope she isn't shaken like Sister Angelique. I could really use her cloak of prayer right about now."

"Oh, you have more than a cloak of prayer covering you, Pastor! Sister Treva has her own way of fighting this war. You couldn't have seen it because you came in through the basement, but she has a whole army of prayer warriors surrounding the church. They have been praying since the wee hours of the morning. Whenever the reporters or naysayers tried to approach, she and her gang of warriors would pray even harder. It's as if they created a hedge around the church. Like God's angels descended directly from heaven to guard the sanctity of the church. That Sister Treva is a warring woman."

"Is that so!" Pastor Devon laughed at the mere thought. "I know one thing for sure, I am glad Sister Treva is in our corner. I would never want to be on her bad side."

"I swear that woman ascends into heaven every night to sit at God's feet. She gets her instructions and then joins us back here on earth to carry out His wishes," Deacon Maurice insisted.

"As crazy as that sounds, Deac, you may be on to something. I have never met anyone as close to God as she is."

"She is a true jewel."

Pastor Devon could hear the praise team beginning to minister. Today, of all days, he could not miss a minute of the praise and worship portion of service. Once Daria left the office to claim her space in the front row, Pastor Devon and Deacon Maurice entered the sanctuary through a door off the Pastor's study. It was a longer way around, but this would ensure Pastor was not distracted by people who would try to talk to him before service. Today, Pastor Devon needed all his focus on God, not the lookie-loos who had gathered in the sanctuary.

"After Lucas and his followers left yesterday, I thought for sure I would be ministering to empty seats today." Pastor Devon whispered to Deacon Maurice as he looked out over the crowd.

"Yeah, but be careful. Once the devil sees how you turn this situation around, he will surely rear his ugly head. You know the Word says to watch and pray. Joshua and I will be watching while you are praying and preaching."

"I appreciate you both. But I know God will not allow any harm to come to us. Nosey or not, these people will hear a word from the Lord."

After a powerful worship experience, Pastor Devon stepped up to the podium. The entire church fell so silent the roaring of the air conditioner was the only thing that could be heard.

"Good afternoon, Faith Hope and Love Church! It is not lost on me that many of you have come just to bear witness to the pastor who's a possible suspect in a murder investigation. Well, take a good look; here I am." The crowd murmured among themselves. "I also know those who are actual members of this fine church came to support their church and their pastor, and for that, I say thank you, and I am forever grateful." An applause erupted from the congregation.

"I am not here to put on a show, so if that's why you are here, I invite you to leave now. Trust me, there will be no hard feelings. But if you came to hear the preached Word, I have a message to share," more applause erupted from the crowd, along with several "Amens."

After the service, Pastor Devon did not shy away from the crowd. He and Lady Daria took their usual post in the fellowship hall like they do every Sunday to greet their fellow church members and guests. Some brushed passed them without any acknowledgment and were notably full of judgment. Others gave them hugs and thanked him for such a powerful Word.

"Pastor Devon, with everything you are going through, for you to preach a message like that, I know you were sent by God. Please let me know if there is anything my family can do to assist you," one parishioner said.

"Can you believe him, calling himself a man of God! He is a blemish to the office of Pastor," whispered one of the visitors.

Daria held Devon's hand even tighter when she heard the negative venom being spewed. He looked at her with a smile to reassure her everything would be just fine, even if he did not fully believe it himself.

Attorney Harris shook the Pastor's hand and greeted Lady Daria. "Great Word today, Pastor! It was really inspiring to watch you preach with such conviction."

"When you feel as though you are running for your life, sometimes conviction is all you have," Devon replied.

"Do you and Lady Daria have some time Tuesday morning? I am still gathering data, but I would like to stop by and talk to you both about the latest updates."

"Yes, we will be staying at an undisclosed location," Pastor said as he looked around at the ear hustlers nearby. "I will text you the information. Should I include the rest of the team?"

"Let me talk to just the two of you first, and then if you want to bring the others in, it will be your call to make."

"Understood. Let's meet at 10 a.m. Tuesday morning if that works."

"Works for me...I will see you then."

Daria's mind was spinning out of control, and her heart was beating rapidly. Devon could sense she was struggling, so he cut his greetings with the visitors and members short. He gave a little tug on her hand for her to follow him into his study.

"Baby...I know you are trying to be strong for me. But I need you to talk to me. Do you need to go to Virginia with the kids and our parents?"

"No, I wouldn't dare leave your side while you are dealing with this storm. We are in this together. I may get a bit emotional from time to time, but I am still standing."

"You are such an empath. I know your emotions are where you draw your strength. I understand, and I love you so much," Devon pulled her into his arms.

"It's just sometimes the accusations and negativity are too much. I cannot bear the thought of losing you."

"Losing me? You are never going to lose me," he pulled back from her to look into her eyes. "Before we talk about losing anybody, let's see what Attorney Harris says. I feel uneasy about it, but I will not jump to conclusions, and you can't either."

"I know..." she began but was interrupted.

"No, baby, I need you to hear me. I know you know I couldn't have done what they are accusing me of, but we also know the justice system. Whatever happens, I need you to be strong. And if I am arrested, for some unforeseeable reason, I need you to stay with your parents because I don't want you here alone."

"But Devon..."

"No buts, I am serious. I cannot see myself in a jail cell, but if I must be, I can survive better knowing you are not alone. You must promise me, baby."

"Yes, I cannot fathom you being arrested, but heaven forbid, if it happens, I will go to my parents to be with the kids."

The couple held each other in a long passionate embrace while tears streamed down their faces.

"I will always love you, Daria."

"And I will always love you, Devon."

Chapter 8

*A*ngelique Dobson sat nervously in the waiting room of the Charlotte Police Station where Detectives Johnston and Sneed worked. She felt as though she was betraying her Pastor and the entire church congregation by being here, but what harm could it cause? She was simply asked by the Detectives to come down to see some pictures of the deceased, Jocelyn Brandon. Being the church administrator, she knew most of the comings and goings in the church. She certainly recorded the names of everyone who needed to get in to see the Pastor.

"Ms. Dobson, follow me, please." Detective Johnston's presence in the lobby startled her. Angelique's thoughts had momentarily blocked out her surroundings. As she stood to follow him, Brother Lucas quickly skirted past them at a quick pace. His head was down, but she recognized him immediately. That unsettling feeling intensified from wondering if she was doing the right thing being there. She was asked not to mention her appointment to the Pastor and church leaders. She obeyed so as not to get into legal trouble, but her spirit was not at peace. Detective Johnston led Angelique to a conference room where Detective Sneed and Lead Detective Ramsey gathered.

"Hello, Ms. Dobson. I am Lead Detective Joe Ramsey. It is nice to meet you."

"Hello," she managed, feeling a bit intimidated by the energy in the room. Detective Johnston was nice enough, and Detective Ramsey seemed very pleasant. Still, there was a scowl coming from Detective Sneed, which gave her an uneasy feeling.

"Thank you for taking time this morning to meet with us," Detective Ramsey continued. "Please, have a seat.

"Thank you," she replied. As she sat at the table, Detective Sneed waddled over with two manilla folders in his hands.

"Look, let's get right to it. We need to know if you recognize this woman." He demanded while opening one of the folders and shoving the contents before her.

She looked at him for a moment, trying to get a read on him, then she dropped her gaze to the folders opened in front of her. She winced at the images she saw. Immediately turning away, she looked at Detective Ramsey as tears began to form in her eyes, and a look of horror covered her face."

I'm so sorry, Ms. Dobson." Detective Ramsey interjected, apologizing for Detective Sneed's rude behavior, "Sneed! Johnston and I will handle things from here."

"But sir...," Sneed began.

"Out Sneed!" Ramsey demanded.

Once Detective Sneed left the room, Detective Ramsey turned his attention back to Angelique, who sat visibly shaken. "Again, I am so sorry. He had no business showing you those photographs. That is not what we discussed, and he will be reprimanded." Ramsey quickly closed the folder containing pictures from the crime scene, grabbed it, and forcefully pushed it into Detective Johnston's chest. Johnston took the hint and left the room, nodding to Angelique before exiting. Ramsey opened the remaining folder containing pictures from Jocelyn's family home. "These are the pictures we wanted you to see. Have you ever seen this woman?"

Slowly Angelique's gaze dropped from Detective Ramsey to the pictures laid out in front of her. The images on top were of Jocelyn at her prom and high school graduation. There were more recent pictures of her on vacation at the beach and what appeared to be a celebration. She was a beautiful woman. Her long black hair was pulled into a beautiful bun with the front neatly styled in a razor-sharp Chinese bob with longer strands of hair on both sides of her face. Her skin was flawless, and her smile was mesmerizing. Angelique shuffled through a few more of the pictures before her. Then she landed on one where Jocelyn wore a red wig. This picture caught her attention. Before realizing it, she blurted out, "It's her. This is her!"

"Who, Ms. Dobson?" inquired Detective Ramsey.

"Oh, I'm sorry. I do recognize her. She seemed somewhat familiar in the other pictures, but this one specifically. This is the woman who came to the church in a panic. She is the one from that night."

"The night you and Deacon Maurice called Pastor Royce to the church?"

Realizing she may have just betrayed her Pastor; she simply nodded her head.

"Ms. Dobson, in most instances, I understand you are bound by confidentiality; but you may be holding important evidence needed to solve this case." Detective Ramsey walked to the conference room door and waved for Johnston to come back in. He walked back over to Angelique. "Tell us everything that happened from the time she arrived at the church."

Angelique sighed. She knew she had to oblige as this could be vital to solving the case. Before speaking, she asked for a glass of water and a moment to compose her thoughts. After getting her a cup of water, both men left the room to give her a few minutes to compose herself.

Angelique wrestled with what she should or should not say. She knew she had to tell the police about that night, but it could potentially make her dear pastor look even more suspect. The fact that Brother Lucas was also questioned was not good. She realized others would be called in for questioning as well. She said a little prayer for God to give her what to say so as not to incriminate Pastor Devon.

When the detectives came back, they had a female officer with them. She had a recording device, pens, and notepads. Angelique's anxiety level peaked at the thought of her words being recorded. She was somewhat relieved when she noticed Detective Sneed was not with them. This made the tension in the room a little lighter. Once everything was set up, Detective Ramsey asked Angelique to state her name, the date and time of the incident in question, and the details surrounding the encounter with Jocelyn.

Angelique looked up towards the ceiling and then redirected her gaze to Detective Ramsey. "My name is Angelique Dobson. I am the church administrator for Faith Hope and Love Church. On Thursday, May 18, 2022, I was finishing up some work in my office at the church." She glanced at the faces in the room, each of which was staring intently back at her.

She continued, "I heard a commotion in the lobby, so I walked out to see what was happening. A young woman walked in crying and screaming, "Where is he? Where is the pastor?" Brother Lucas and Deacon Maurice were with her at the time. I walked over to see if I could help calm her so we could determine how we could be of assistance to her. She kept looking back at the front door as if she expected someone to come in at any minute. For her safety, Deacon Maurice and I walked her to Pastor Devon's office. Brother Lucas went to grab her a bottle of water."

"Was someone after her?" Detective Johnston interrupted.

"I don't know. The entire interaction was odd."

"Did she give you her name?" Detective Ramsey chimed in.

"Yes, well, sort of. When I asked her name, she said it was Trini. She wouldn't give me a last name. I assumed 'Trini' was a nickname or short for something else."

"Continue with the story, please." Ramsey glanced over the notes he had already scribed, excited to connect this to the young lady found dead.

"So, Trini finally calmed down after drinking a few sips of water. She finished wiping her tears and blowing her nose with the tissue I provided her. She did not want to talk to me or Deacon Maurice. She insisted on speaking directly to the Pastor of the church, so I asked Deacon if he would give Pastor Devon a call."

"When Pastor arrived, Trini was much calmer than when she first appeared in the church lobby. He seemed to have recognized her but did not mention anything to Deacon or me. He said everything was okay and motioned for Deacon and me to step out. We complied."

"It seems the Pastor may have recognized the woman?" Johnston reiterated.

"Yes. I mean, he didn't say as much, but it was something about Pastor's expression that led me to think he had seen her before."

"How long were they in the office alone?" asked Ramsey.

"I don't know, maybe ten or fifteen minutes. It seemed as if everything was under control. At least until just before she stormed out."

"Wait, she stormed out? Do you know why?" an engaged Ramsey inquired.

"I don't really know. I just know voices grew louder in the office. I couldn't make out what was said, but I could hear the conversation growing louder. Moments after, Pastor's door flung open, and I could see he was trying to escort her out. She was screaming, '*You are going to pay for this!*' It caught us all off guard. I couldn't imagine what she meant by that or how she and Pastor Devon were even acquainted."

"When you say we, you are referring to you, Deacon Maurice, and Brother Lucas?"

"Yes, we were all in my office across the hall from Pastor's office. What was worse, she slapped Pastor Devon before grabbing her purse and storming out of the church."

"Brother Lucas and I followed her out to ensure she left the premises, and we locked the door once she exited. Deacon Maurice walked with Pastor to the basement exit door in the back of the church. Only a few of us use that door or even know about it. We use it when we want to slip in and out of the church without being stopped or interrupted."

"Ok, so did Pastor Royce say anything to any of you before he left? Did he give any explanation?" Johnston questioned.

"Not to Brother Lucas or me. When we returned to the office, he and Deacon had left."

"Is there anything more you remember from that night, Ms. Dobson?

"No, not that I can recall. I have shared with you everything I know. None of us knew that Trini's real name was Jocelyn. Pastor Devon did not lie about that."

"Her full name is Jocelyn Katrina Brandon. Maybe "Trini" is a short name for Katrina."

"Those gruesome pictures Detective Sneed placed in front of me did not look like the woman you showed me in the pictures. I only recognized her from the picture of her with the red wig on. It was the same wig she wore that night. Look, I don't know what happened after she left the church, but I do know my Pastor, and I know he could not have possibly done anything to hurt her. He is not a violent man." The female officer stopped the tape and began gathering the items she had brought into the room.

"For your Pastor's sake, I hope you are right. Ms. Dobson, thank you for taking the time to interview with us. This information is helpful. I assure you we will sort this out."

Everyone stood up, and Ramsey extended his hand to Angelique. She shook his hand and was led out of the room and back to the lobby.

"We need to have another conversation with the good Pastor and Deacon Maurice. The conversation in the office could lead to Pastor Royce's motive for wanting to harm her." Detective Johnston presumptuously concluded.

"I agree, we need to talk with both gentlemen, but an argument alone is not enough motive to kill. We need to find out how Pastor Royce knew Jocelyn and what led up to her slapping and threatening him. Call Deacon Maurice first. They should be out of the church by now. Let's see what Pastor Royce confided in him as they walked to the car."

"I'm on it, sir. Do you want me to bring Sneed up to speed?"

"No, Sneed is not in a good headspace now. We don't need his bull-in-a-China shop mentality to impede any parts of this investigation. Partner up with Evans on this one. I'll deal with Sneed."

"Yes sir."

Chapter 9

Chapter 9

*A*fter service, Joshua and Stephanie drove the Royce's' home to pick up their car. Devon and Daria followed them to a rural area just a few miles outside city limits. They pulled up to a whimsical storybook cottage with elaborate trim, window boxes lined with greenery and flowers, and a blue arched door. The picturesque home was surrounded by lush, tall mature trees.

"Wow, man! You did say it was off the grid," Devon said as both men exited their cars. Devon could not help but admire the cottage as he walked to the passenger side to open the door for Daria.

"Yeah, I dabble in real estate. Steph and I ran across this baby and couldn't bear to flip it. We decided to keep it for special occasions, our ideal adventurous hideaway," Joshua added as he licked his lips and winked at his wife. Melting by his smile, she blew a sweet kiss his way.

"Awwww...get a room," Devon teased.

"Honey, they have a whole cottage," Daria chimed in. Both couples laughed as they exited the car and followed the natural stone pathway to the front door. "It's so peaceful," Daria whispered and lost herself as the aroma of roses being carried by the wind tickled her nose. As she glanced at the thick blades of grass, it looked like a vast velvety green carpet inviting her to remove her shoes and take a stroll on the lawn. "Look at these flowers," she said, pointing to the brilliant shades of marigolds in the flower beds. It was all too much to take in. She closed her eyes as if they were shutters on a camera capturing each moment and storing them for later.

Inside the cottage was a visually pleasing design of elegant meets modern meets serene, yet it maintained a timeless charm. Devon and Daria entered the kitchen and the dining area from the comfortable and inviting living room.

"Baby, look at this!" Daria exclaimed.

"Wait, there is a pond in the backyard? Dude, you didn't tell me you had it like this," teased Devon.

"Well, it's not actually in the backyard, but it is close enough to enjoy from the deck. This is our oasis. The sounds, the smell, the cool breeze, all of it helps us wind down. We love it here."

"We are honored you and Steph are sharing it with us," Daria responded.

After acclimating to their new surroundings, Joshua and Stephanie left to give them some alone time. Devon and Daria decided to take advantage of the alone time. Instead of rallying the troops or trying to figure out their next move, they decided to have a quiet evening at the cottage. Stephanie had Instacart deliver groceries for them so they could settle in. Daria wanted to take Devon's mind off his predicament and escape reality herself, so she cooked his favorite grilled steak and loaded mashed potatoes. She. Daria served the romantic dinner on the deck of the beautiful cottage. Smooth jazz, the evening breeze, a glass of red wine, and the company of each other were all either of them wanted to place their focus on. Neither of them was big on drinking, but an occasional glass of wine would not hurt anything. They needed the relaxation it would bring.

"Baby, this was a wonderful idea. Thank you for always knowing what I need even before I do." Devon said as he glanced over at his beautiful wife. The radiance of the golden sunset on her beautiful bronze skin made her glow. He always felt his wife was gorgeous, but in this setting, she was breathtaking.

Daria feeling a little flirtatious, looked up at her husband with a provocative glance. "Well, you know, this is not the only thing I know you need." She said sheepishly.

"Is that so?"

"Why don't you come over here so I can show you what else you need." Daria rose from her seat and headed backward step-by-step towards the hot tub while keeping her eyes locked on Devon. She had already turned on the heated jets while cooking dinner to ensure everything would be perfect for this special moment. Pieces of clothing fell at her feet as she continued to stroll. Pants, blouse, black-laced satin bra, and panties created a pathway for her husband to follow. Devon felt his longing for Daria grow intensely. He loved how she aroused him and marveled at her sexiness. His eyes followed her body until she was fully submerged in the tub. Then he quickly began removing his clothes and joined her. They spent hours kissing, caressing, and satisfying each other. Meeting and exceeding every physical and emotional need. Once they left the comfort of the hot tub, they toweled each other dry and made their way to the bedroom. There was no sleep for them as the bedroom only refueled their fire. The night was all about pleasure as a husband pleased his wife and a wife pleased her husband. They delved into one another like it was their first time making love. Both enjoyed the exploration, the climax, and the release encapsulating the obvious love and passion between them. At some point, they both drifted into a deep sleep in each other's arms. It was the best sleep either of them had in some time.

Their embrace was interrupted as Devon's phone rang. It was preset to go on do not disturb at night. Before things ignited between him and Daria the night before, he had extended the time of the do not disturb feature to 11 a.m. Even before things heated up, he knew he wanted to sleep in. He was happier than ever for his preplanning. But 11 a.m. came, and his phone was ringing non-stop. He did not answer the first time it rang, but it rang back-to-back, so he knew it had to be urgent.

He slowly pulled away from his beautiful wife as she continued to lay peacefully beside him. He grabbed the phone from the nightstand and went into the bathroom. He saw Angelique's name on the screen. "Hi, Angelique," he began.

"Pastor, I have something important to tell you. I have been trying to call all morning."

"What is it? What's wrong?"

"Pastor, do you remember the young lady Deacon Maurice asked you to meet Friday night?

"Yes, what about her?"

"Pastor, that's Jocelyn Brandon! She told us her name was Trini, but it is the same person!"

"What!" Devon exclaimed.

Startled by the outburst, Daria woke up. "Devon, what's wrong?"

"Where did you hear this?" Devon continued with the conversation ignoring his wife for the moment.

"Pastor, I know you noticed I wasn't at church yesterday."

"Of course, I noticed; we all did."

"It was because I was asked to come to the police station to view photos of the girl who was murdered."

"What!" Devon exclaimed again, pacing back and forth from the bathroom to the master bedroom.

"Yes, they asked me to come in yesterday morning. I was instructed not to say anything to anyone. I thought I would simply go in and tell them I have never seen that woman before, which would release you from any connection with her. They showed me her pictures at the crime scene, which will haunt me for a long time. But then, they showed me pictures of her before she was murdered. I didn't recognize her in a few of the pictures because her hair and makeup were different. Still, there was one picture …" Angelique drifted off. "It was unmistakable. Trini and Jocelyn are the same person! Trini is short for her middle name, which is Katrina."

"Pastor, what happened in your office that night? What made her so angry with you?"

"Angelique, give me a little time to process all of this. Gather everyone together this afternoon. I will fill everyone in when we meet."

"Yes sir, Pastor."

"Devon, what on earth is going on? You look like you've seen a ghost."

"Baby, sit down."

"Don't tell me to sit down; tell me what's going on!" Daria insisted.

"Something happened the other night when I left you and the kids and went to the church."

"Something? Something like what?"

"I didn't tell you because I didn't think anything of it."

"Stop being vague and tell me, Devon!"

"There was a lady who came to the church. She was borderline hysterical. That's why Deac called me in. He said there was some inconsolable woman who insisted on speaking with me."

"Who was this woman, and why did she need to speak to you specifically? There are other people at the church trained in de-escalation."

"I know. The woman wanted me specifically because she thought I was someone else. It was a case of mistaken identity."

"This doesn't make sense, Devon. What aren't you telling me?"

"Ok...just let me explain. When I got to the church, she was already sitting in my office. She said her name was Trini. I recognized her because I had seen her on the church premises recently. I tried to go over and speak to her, but she would take off. I found it strange but thought nothing more of it. I went into the office, and she told me she was pregnant and accused me of being the father."

Suddenly, Daria's whole demeanor changed. Devon could not tell how she was processing what she had heard thus far. "Baby, look at me." Devon pleaded. "It is not my baby. I have never and will never cheat on you. You've got to believe me."

"I don't know what to believe," Daria broke her silence. "Some woman accuses you of impregnating her, and you didn't think that was worthy of sharing with me the same night? Who is this woman? Why would she accuse you of getting her pregnant?"

"Baby, my hand to God, it was not me! I didn't tell you because I didn't want to upset you. Clearly a poor decision on my part. She and I got into an argument when I told her the baby wasn't mine, and I have never ever put one hand on her. She started cursing and calling me out of my name. Before she left my office, she slapped me and said she would make me pay for this.

"Devon! What the hell have you done—did you kill this woman?"

"Daria! How dare you ask me that! You know me! You know I could never kill anyone!"

"Then explain to me how a woman who says you slept together, and she is having your baby ends up dead! How the hell does that happen? Sounds more than coincidental to me!"

"Daria! What are you saying?"

"I'm saying I can understand why the police see you as a person of interest. If they know any of this, then it stands to reason you are a primary suspect!"

"Daria! It wasn't me. The fact you are insinuating I could cheat on you or kill someone is pissing me off! I won't stand for your accusations!"

"Pissing you off? Devon, you went against our vows and against God! How could you?"

Devon quickly grabbed his overnight bag sitting on the closet floor. He slammed the bedroom door as he stormed out. He went into the downstairs bathroom to change into his sweats. Daria followed him downstairs. She banged on the bathroom door. Devon opened the door, pushed passed her, and bolted for the front door.

"Where do you think you are going?" Daria demanded in a shrilling tone.

"Anywhere but here! You know I am not a cheater or a murderer! I cannot believe you would think any of this was true!"

"You aren't giving me any reason to think otherwise!"

"Damn! *Fifteen* years of marriage is your reason to think otherwise!"

Devon stomped past Daria out of the bathroom. His anger had escalated by the time he grabbed the front door handle, pulling it with such force it hit the stopper and bounced back into his hand, after which he slammed the door behind him. Daria stared at the door as though she was waiting for the entire scene to rewind so she could press 'play' and change what had just happened. But seeing her husband leave in sudden fury and recalling her accusations of infidelity and murder was far too overwhelming. Tears flooded her eyes, and she began sobbing hysterically. She ran upstairs and threw herself on the bed, crying until she could hardly catch her breath. "How could he do this to me?" She wailed and sunk her face into the satin comforter screaming and beating her fists on the bed where they had spent such a magical night just hours before.

Devon drove down the highway, aware he was speeding but not in control enough to slow down. He had no destination; he just had to get away. If Daria doesn't believe him, how could anyone else be expected to do so? He didn't know what angered him most. Was it her insinuation of infidelity, the accusation of murder, Daria not believing in him, or his dwindling faith in God to be delivered from this storm? "God!" He yelled. "What the hell? Why have you forsaken me?"

Before he knew it, Devon found himself parked in front of one of the bars not far from the cottage. He pondered calling Joshua but decided against it. Instead, he went into the establishment and right up to the bar.

"What will it be?" the bartender asked.

"What?" Devon sounded confused.

"Did you want to order something? Man, are you ok?

"Yeah, I'll have a whiskey on the rocks."

"Coming up." The bartender poured the brown liquor into a glass filled with ice and set it in front of Devon. Before he could take a sip, his phone rang. Joshua was calling him. 'Had Daria told them about the argument?' Regardless, Devon answered the call.

"Yeah," he answered.

"Hey, brother! What's the move for today? What did Rich have to say?" Sensing something was not quite right, he added, "You good, dude?"

"Honestly? No, I am anything but good!"

"Dude...what happened?"

"It's too much to discuss over the phone."

"Do you want me and Stephanie to come over? We got a strange call from Angelique stating we all needed to meet."

"No, I'm not at the cottage. I am at the Whiskey Bar."

"The Whiskey Bar? But you don't drink." Joshua sensed an intervention was needed when he did not receive a response. "Man, what the hell? Don't drink anything more than water or sweet tea. I am not far from you; I am on my way."

Devon hung up the call and sat gazing at his drink. He thought to himself, "What's happening to me? How could one strange encounter change the course of my life?" He looked in the mirror on the wall behind the bar. Just above the sea of alcohol, he saw his reflection, yet he barely recognized himself. He sat in a daze staring at the stranger's reflection in the mirror, until his thoughts were interrupted by someone calling his name.

"Devon!" Joshua blurted out as he made his way to the bar. Devon looked up but did not respond.

"My man..." Joshua lifted his hand to get the bartender's attention. Pointing to the drink in front of Devon, he asked, "How many of these has he had?"

"He barely took a sip of that one. He's just been sitting there in a daze."

"Thank you." He paid Devon's tab and grabbed him by the arm. "Come on, man, this is no place for you. Let's go to the basketball court and talk this out. We can take your car and come back for mine later."

Joshua would much rather have someone identify his car at the bar than have Devon's car recognized. When they arrived at the courts, the lot was empty. Joshua pulled into a spot across from the nearest basketball court. Realizing neither of them had a basketball, he turned to Devon in the car. "Dude, what is going on with you? This is completely out of character."

"She doesn't believe me, man. She doesn't believe me!"

"Who doesn't believe you?"

"Dee, man."

"What doesn't she believe? I can't help you if I don't know what's going on."

Devon took a few deep breaths to temper his breathing and calm his nerves. "Angelique called this morning. She confirmed the dead woman was the same woman who came to the church Thursday night. Apparently, Jocelyn and Trini are the same person. Trini is the woman who came to the church. Man...she accused me of having sex with her and getting her pregnant!"

"Wait, hold on. I'm not following."

Devon turned to face his friend. He shared the details of the encounter Thursday night. When he left the church, he went for a drive because he needed to clear his head. Some random woman had accused him of impregnating her.

"Did you know her?"

"No, that's the crazy part. I mean, I saw her a couple of times around the church, but I have never so much as spoken to her."

"Let's think about this, Devon. Why would she accuse you of being the father of her child? I am pretty sure you would both know if you had sex."

"That's the million-dollar question. Apparently, the police are interviewing members of the church. Angelique said she was called in, and while she was there, she saw Lucas leaving. God only knows what he said. Now I look like a liar because she gave us a different name."

"Lucas, what does he know about any of this?"

"Lucas, Angelique, and Deac were all there when the lady came in. I'm sure he heard us arguing in the office and witnessed her slapping me as she stormed out. Oh, and I'm sure he heard her say she would make me pay."

"Dude, this is deep! And you shared this with Lady Daria?"

"Not when it happened, but I did after Angelique's call."

"Dude...wrong move! You should have told her the night it happened. Now you look like you have something to hide."

"I know that now. I just didn't want to upset her. I didn't think it would come back to haunt me, let alone cause my world to implode."

"Let's not panic. I know you, so I know you would never do anything you are being accused of doing. And if we are being honest, Lady Daria knows it as well. She is just hurt at the thought of it. And how she found out, I can understand why she is so upset and not thinking straight. You both are going through one of the worst storms of your life. Your emotions are on edge, but she will come around, man. She loves you too much to believe any of this nonsense."

"From your lips to God's ears, man."

"God knows exactly what happened. He knows our deepest darkest secrets. You seem to have favor with the Big Guy, so I am pretty sure He will get you through this. Just have faith."

"You are right. I know better, but when you are going through character assassination, it's a little hard to stand on faith. But you are right. I have a lot of apologizing to do, starting with the Big Guy."

"Dude, the bar though?" Both men laughed.

"Let's keep this between us."

"My man!"

Chapter 10

$\mathcal{D}$aria, emotionally exhausted, called her mother. "Mama, you are not going to believe this."

"What is it, baby?" Mother Hendrix asked, hearing the pain in her daughter's voice.

"Mama, Devon just told me some lady came to the church last week with accusations that he was her baby's daddy!"

"Daria, really? I find that hard to believe."

"And to make matters worse, this is the same woman who was found dead a short time later."

"Daria, listen to what you are saying. Surely you do not believe Devon would step out on you. And we both know he is not a murderer. I need you to get a hold of yourself. Think about what you are saying."

"But Mama, he did not tell me about this lady. He must be hiding something!"

"Daria, honey, where is he now?"

"We got into a huge argument, and he stormed out."

"Baby, I love you, but let's face it. Sometimes you can let your imagination get the best of you. You are a creative spirit, and sometimes you allow that creativity to fuel some wild imaginations. I know all men have it in them to cheat, but that does not mean they all act on that instinct. Some men know how to exercise restraint, and Devon has proven himself to be one of them. I have seen how Devon is with you. He loves you more than life itself. You are letting the devil take residence in that beautiful little head of yours. Have you sought God on any of this, or did you just go into hysterics when you heard about it?"

"I cannot believe you don't have my back on this. How could some woman accuse him of getting her pregnant if they had not slept together first?"

"Remember the Garden of Eden and how the serpent came in and twisted the truth for his pleasure? He had Eve believing a truth that didn't exist. That is the way satan tries to destroy us. He will play on our emotions and weaknesses and make us second-guess things we otherwise know are true. Now I don't have an answer as to why this woman accused him of getting her pregnant, but I do know it is tied to the lie about him murdering her. I am pretty sure if one is a lie, both are a lie. Everything is not always as it is perceived. Look past your emotions and stand on what you know."

"Of course, I know he isn't a murderer. But Mama, I am having a hard time with the infidelity piece, and why wouldn't he tell me when she first accused him?"

"Because men are protectors by nature. In his mind, not bringing this to you was his way of protecting you. I don't believe he was hiding anything; I think he used poor judgment in not telling you before now. If you want to charge him for anything, charge him for being a man. They just don't think like we think. You said you know he isn't a murderer; did you tell him that?"

"I did when he was first accused, but to be honest, while we were arguing, I did ask him if he killed her.

"Now Daria!"

"I know, Mama. I owe him an apology. I guess you are right. I mean, I never once worried about him being unfaithful in the fifteen years we've been married, or the two years we dated before that."

"So why believe such an accusation without proof now? It's one thing if you had solid proof he cheated on you, but just to go by the word of a random woman; I raised you to be smarter than that. Follow what you know, not what is perceived."

"Mama, you are right. Oh goodness, I flat-out accused him to his face. I did not for one second think it could be a lie. How will he ever forgive me? How am I going to fix this?"

"That man loves your stinky little panties...I'm sure he will have no problem forgiving you. He is a wise man. Even in the heat of battle, I know cooler heads will prevail for both of you. Calm down and really think about it all. You will see how the enemy tried to rear its ugly head."

"You are right, Mama, and what you said makes sense. Thank you for talking me off the ledge. I don't know what I would do without you. How do you stay so calm and graceful?"

"Years of being humbled by God. If I haven't learned anything else, I have learned that God will humble you."

"I love you, Mama. Thank you for being such a strong example for me."

"I love you, too, baby. Now get off this phone and go makeup with that husband of yours. Tell him your Daddy, and I are praying for you both. Neither of us believes these accusations for one moment. And Daria, no matter what else you hear, if you do not have solid facts to back it up, it's just another lie until it can be proven to be true."

"Yes ma'am. Love you, Mommy. Talk to you later."

"Talk to you later, my love."

Devon dreaded this moment. He received a call from Angelique notifying him that 'the team' had assembled at the church. Rich and Stephanie were not able to leave their perspective jobs but were able to connect through Zoom. Angelique picked Lady Daria up from the cottage and saw her First Lady had been crying. Being a woman, she could only imagine how the conversation went after her call. Angelique felt she had to reassure her of Pastor Devon's innocence. After conversing for an hour, the ladies left for the church. Daria agreed there was no way Devon was the man the police were portraying him to be. She told Angelique she had a conversation with her mother and understood the enemy was just trying to rear its head. Now more than ever, Daria knew to ask her husband for forgiveness. Everything was unraveling before her eyes, and she acted out of emotion, not wisdom, and certainly not faith. She admitted her humanity got in the way of sound judgment. She knew her husband and knew he could never do the things for which he stood accused.

Before they met with everyone else, Daria asked if she could speak with her husband alone first. They went into Devon's office while the rest of the team waited in the fellowship hall.

"Baby..." they both seemed to blurt out in unison.

"No, Devon, let me go first, please." Daria insisted as she stepped closer to her husband, who was leaning against his mahogany desk. "Baby, I was totally wrong. I should have never jumped to conclusions. I know you are a good man. I know you would never cheat on me, and I certainly know you cannot commit murder. I let the enemy get in my head. Can you ever forgive me?"

"Daria, only if you forgive me. I, too, am sorry. I should have come to you when I got home that night and told you everything that transpired. But I thought I was doing the right thing. Now I know I was wrong. I do not blame you for getting upset. I was the one who opened the door for the enemy to attempt to cause division in our marriage. I love you so much, Daria Hendrix-Royce. I would never do anything to ruin what we have." Devon pulled his wife closer to him and embraced her. She could feel the genuineness even through his embrace.

"Now, let's let our friends know what's going on. I have a feeling a few more of them will get requests to be interviewed by the police." Devon grabbed Daria's hand and walked with her to the fellowship hall.

"Thank you for assembling so quickly," Devon began. "I owe each of you an apology...several apologies, if I'm being honest. First, I must apologize for dragging you all into my mess. This is not a normal part of ministry, and I truly would not fault any of you if you wanted to walk away from the madness. Next, I need to apologize for saying I did not know the victim. I honestly had no idea she was the lady who came to the church Thursday night. She came in demanding to see me. When I arrived, she accused me of fathering her child. Before you say anything, I assure you, I only have eyes for this lady right here." He held Daria's hand in his.

"Pastor Devon, I cannot speak for everyone here, but I can speak for Steph and me when I say we are in this with you. We will walk through this fire with you 'til the bitter end." Joshua responded as he looked at the Zoom chat on the computer screen, where his lovely wife nodded her head in agreement.

"I appreciate that, but there is more. The police have questioned Sister Angelique and Brother Lucas." He turned to Angelique, "I know it was an ordeal for you, but let me assure you, you did the right thing. I would not have asked you to say anything different. I don't want you to feel guilty or responsible for anything that happens. I really need you to hear me."

"Yes, Pastor, thank you for saying that," Angelique responded with tears in her eyes.

"Before we go any further, the police reached out to me just before I got here. They want me to come in as well." Deacon Maurice responded. "I wanted to give them a piece of my mind and tell them where they should go, but I didn't."

"Well, I am grateful you didn't. No need for both of us to be wearing matching jumpsuits. I will say the same thing to you as I did to Sister Angelique. I need you to be honest. No point in incriminating yourself on my behalf. If we are honest and cooperative, we will get through this. In total transparency, my faith has been flailing recently. None of us are above attack, and we all are human. I want to publicly apologize to Daria for being in my flesh this morning and failing to tell her about the encounter here at the church with Trini."

"Pastor Devon," Sister Treva chimed in. "You are absolutely correct; we are all human, and sometimes we will act in our humanity over our spirituality. We all fall short of God's glory. The most important thing is for us to recognize when we are allowing our humanity to overpower our judgment."

"Amen, Sister Treva! I don't know what I would do without you. Without any of you, for that matter."

"Pastor Devon," Rich's voice broadcasted through the computer speakers. "I have been working with my team on your case." Everyone's attention focused on the box on the screen that housed Rich's video image. "We have found out more about what the police know. There were three sets of fingerprints on Jocelyn's car door. One set belonged to her, and there were two others they were still trying to identify. From what I hear, there may be two assailants, not one. This actually works in your favor, as we know you were not in cahoots with anyone to kill this young lady. Next, they were able to run a paternity test on the fetus. The baby is definitely not yours."

"Well, praise God for that," Daria blurted out before realizing it. She blushed, and everyone else laughed as they understood her expression of relief.

"I have a feeling she had a male friend, and maybe the two of them were attempting to extort money from you somehow. We still are not sure what she stood to gain by lying about sleeping with you. One of the bullet casings was found at the scene; they are analyzing it as we speak. What we do know for sure is the bullet did not come from your gun. They were able to confirm your weapon has not been fired recently."

Cheers swept through the room. "Praise God indeed!" shouted Deacon Maurice.

"He is worthy, but I don't want to give false hope. We are not out of the woods yet. We still do not have an explanation about the eyewitness sighting or the DNA and fingerprints at the scene. We still have a long way to go before we can truly celebrate."

"You know what...regardless, we will still celebrate the small victories," Devon replied.

"Can't argue with you there, Pastor," Rich agreed. "Don't forget, I still need to meet with you and Lady Daria alone tomorrow morning. We must jump some hurdles before this is all said and done."

"Yes, we will meet you at the cottage tomorrow at 10 a.m.," Devon confirmed.

"Deacon Maurice, please follow up on the interview with the police. I want to get that done before I speak with Pastor Devon tomorrow. Please let us know if there is anything you know that has not already been laid out on the table. We really don't need any more surprises," Rich's look was serious, and his tone was stern. The team could tell they were not out of the woods yet. Not by a long shot.

"I don't know anything the rest of you don't already know. At least not at this point. I am curious to know who these eyewitnesses are and what Lucas said during his interview. But as soon as I finish my interview, I will reach out to let you all know what happened."

Chapter 11

*W*hile landscaping around the cottage, Joshua saw a car pulling up. He knew it was Attorney Harris. He walked over to greet him.

"Hi, Josh," Attorney Harris said as he exited his car.

"Hey, Rich."

"Wow, this is beyond beautiful. I had no idea all of this was out here."

"That's the idea," Joshua replied as he shook Rich's hand.

"Come on in. I was just finishing up." Joshua opened the door to allow Rich to enter. He turned to Devon. "I will head out to give you guys your privacy. Feel free to give us a call if you need anything."

"Have a seat, Rich," Devon said as he returned to the living room. "We have been on pins and needles waiting for this conversation."

Daria walked in with an ice-cold pitcher of sweet tea and three glasses. "Sorry I can't offer more, but I haven't had a chance to whip up anything, Rich."

"No problem, I understand." As Daria poured sweet tea into each of the three glasses, Rich pulled out his briefcase to review his notes.

"Devon, let me get right to it. There were eyewitnesses, a guy named Nathan Hatcher and his wife, Gloria, who swear they saw you the night the victim, Jocelyn Brandon, who we now know as Trini, was murdered."

Devon turned to his wife with a puzzled look. "Nathan and Gloria Hatcher? Dee, do we know Nathan and Gloria Hatcher?"

"Nathan and Gloria's names ring a bell, but I am not sure where we know them from. They aren't members of the church," she responded.

"Who the Hatchers are isn't the focus right now. What is important is they claim to know you and to have seen you arguing with Ms. Brandon on the night of the murder. According to their account, they were coming out of one of the bars in Uptown Charlotte. They heard a man and a woman arguing as they walked through the parking garage to get into their car."

"What! Why would I be in a parking lot arguing with a woman I don't really know?" Devon interrupted.

Rich glanced at his notes to make sure he conveyed the details correctly. "The witness report said they didn't know the young lady, but they recognized you from the church billboards and social media advertisements. From what they could hear, the person they identified as you seemed upset because this Ms. Brandon told you...him...the assailant, she was pregnant. They heard a little of the conversation but did not see who was talking until they got closer to their car."

Daria was in shock; she could not believe her ears. She felt numb as she shook her head and rocked back and forth. "No, no, this isn't happening. This makes no sense. None of this seems real."

"Baby, it wasn't me. You know that, right? It wasn't me," the humanity in Devon pleaded as he helplessly watched his wife falling apart.

"I don't mean to upset you, Daria. I will stop if you need me to," Rich said, sympathetic to her pain.

"No, I just find all this hard to believe. I'm sorry for my outburst. Please continue."

"That's because it isn't believable," Devon said as he handed Daria the glass of sweet tea sitting in front of her. He didn't want to put Daria through any more of this, but they needed to know what they were up against. He paused the conversation until Daria gave the sign she was okay to continue. She recalled her mother's words: "No matter what else you hear, if you do not have solid facts to back it up, it's just another lie until it can be proven to be true."

"Rich, please go on," she said after she took a few sips of the tea Devon handed her.

Rich looked at Devon to make sure it was okay to continue. Devon gave a slight head nod.

"So apparently, the assailant was angry because Ms. Brandon was pregnant. She wasn't happy with his response to the news, so she went into a blind rage and started hitting him. He grabbed her to calm her down, but she continued to wave her arms wildly. The struggle must have caused them both to lose balance and fall to the ground. Because the Hatchers' said when they were in eye range, they saw the assailant kneeling beside Ms. Brandon. He shook her violently, trying to get her to wake up. He could see her chest moving up and down, so he knew she was still alive but unconscious. They then saw him make a call and put her into the backseat of her car. Or at least the assumption was that it was her car as he appeared to ravage through her purse looking for the keys. They did not want to be spotted, so they got into their car and left."

"Okay, so the Hatchers heard an altercation and witnessed a man putting her in the back seat of her car. But based on what you just said, the young lady was unconscious but still alive," Devon reiterated, playing the story back in his mind.

"Yes, but shortly after, the young lady's car was found abandoned. It had crashed on a back road, and her body was lying on the ground only a few feet away with a gunshot to her stomach. Ironically, she was only a mile or so from the hospital," Rich paused so the couple could digest everything being said.

"If there was a struggle, wouldn't my husband also have scratches or bruises on him if he was the assailant?" Daria asked, making air quotes with her fingers.

"Yes, that is true, Lady Daria. I brought that up to the D.A. handling the case. It seems they have some evidence, but it's all circumstantial. Of course, you know they have your clothing and gun, which all corroborate your side of the story. But from the church office, they found a tissue and a water bottle. I presume this will confirm Trini and Jocelyn are indeed one and the same. Nothing surprising there. However, they are also waiting for the DNA reports to return and fingerprints from the car. There appear to be three sets of fingerprints and skin and hair particles found under Jocelyn's fingernails."

"I had nothing to do with this. Once that is established, how do we figure out who really killed this young lady?" Devon inquired.

"Great question. It's hard to say, but I must believe the results will take the heat off you, and maybe this person or persons have priors which would mean their prints are in the police database. This will make it a lot easier to ID the true assailants."

"Okay then, it sounds bad, but the three of us here know Devon is innocent." Daria asserted, assuring Devon they were a unified front. "It seems all they have is circumstantial evidence."

"Here is where it gets tricky. Because they have eyewitnesses and video from the parking lot cameras, the police feel they have enough to bring charges against you, Devon. They are close to issuing an arrest warrant."

"*WHAT! NO!*" Daria screamed.

"Video footage of me? Arrest warrant?" Devon asked in disbelief.

"Unfortunately, the person in the video does look a lot like you, Devon. From the angle, it did not catch the full encounter, but it did catch the assailant removing his phone from his ear and putting the young lady in the back of her car. It also caught him rummaging through her purse, looking for the keys."

"I swear that's just not possible!"

"Look, I know this isn't the news you wanted to hear, but I must let you know what you are up against. As I said, a warrant will be issued for your arrest by the end of the week. We must get ahead of that."

Devon and Daria looked at each other, sensing what was coming next.

"If you voluntarily turn yourself in, it will look better for your case. It would be an overnight stay, but your bail hearing will be the following morning."

"I can't believe what I am hearing! You mean you want me to turn myself in for a crime I didn't commit?"

"I know it doesn't sound like it is a good thing, but I promise you it will look better if the cops don't have to come hunting for you. Because you don't have any prior offenses, we can get you a reduced bail, and you will then be out until the arraignment hearing."

Devon turned to Daria. Before he could speak, he saw the fear mixed with tears in her eyes. But he also saw her strength. "Baby, I know this is hard, but Rich has a point. If they are after me anyway, I would much rather walk through the doors of the police station on my own than have them arrest and humiliate me in public."

"My faith in God is strong. I know He doesn't give us more than we can bear, but He can't possibly believe I can bear this!" Daria exclaimed.

"Rich, can you call Joshua and Stephanie? I need them to know what is happening. I need them to come and pick up Daria before I turn myself in. She can't be alone."

"Devon..." Daria began.

"No, Daria! You cannot talk me out of this. If one night in a holding cell is what it takes to get me closer to clearing my name, then that's what I will do. I need you to let me do this. Josh and Steph will take good care of you."

"This doesn't have to happen tonight. Since the arrest warrant hasn't been issued yet, Devon has a couple of days before turning himself in. Take the first part of the week to spend time together. I will gather more information and a definitive date on when the warrant will be issued. Once the judge signs it, they have up to three months to execute it. I am quite certain they will not waste much time, though." Turning to Devon, he added, "Let's plan to have you turn yourself in no later than Thursday. If we wait until Friday, you will have to spend the entire weekend in jail, and none of us want that. The process takes a few days. I want you two to spend as much time together as you can. Try to do something to take your mind off what's going on. I know it won't be easy, but that's my recommendation."

"Easier said than done, brother." Devon sighed.

"Daria, if you want, once it's time for his bail hearing, I can pick you up," Rich offered.

"Is that really a good idea, Rich?" Devon wondered.

"Yes, I think so. It may be hard for Daria to see you in the jumpsuit and cuffs, but it will only be until your bail is set. Even though this is a first offense, I would imagine with the charge being murder, it would land your bail around $500,000, which means you would need $50,000 to be released."

"Fifty thousand dollars!" Devon was stunned, and Daria's cries grew louder.

"Are you able to cover the bail? I know it's a lot. I will do all I can to help, but we will have to have it if you can walk out after the hearing."

"Where are we going to get $50,000?" Daria asked. "We have a nice savings but putting that much up would bankrupt us."

"Don't you guys still own property in Virginia?" Rich asked.

"Well, we do have our house we are renting out. My father is overseeing the rental, Devon responded.

"Will that work?" Daria asked.

"Yes, that should cover you. As long as you guys don't leave North Carolina, especially Pastor Devon, the bail will be returned to you after the trial or after he is proven innocent."

"Can you give me time to call my father, Rich? I need to let him know what is going on and have him expedite mailing the deed to the house."

"Yes, that is an excellent idea. I don't want you to turn yourself in until we know we have the money in hand to bail you out. We don't want any hiccups with that."

"Good point."

"Once you have the deed in your hands, let me know. We can plan to go to the police station later this week. Take the first half of the week to rest. Do not conduct any church business and limit your conversations to only 'the team.'

157

My guess was after you shared this with us, your plan was to drive me to the police station?"

"Yes, unfortunately, that was my initial plan. That's why I didn't want to have the others around. But it makes more sense to give you time with your lovely wife. You need a couple of days to get your affairs in order. Once you get everything together, I will be back to pick you up. I want to take you because I have connections there. Considering the circumstances, I want to ensure you are in good hands."

"I understand."

"I will wait until tomorrow to contact 'the team.' We will need our prayer circle around us now more than we ever have before," Daria said, still in disbelief.

Chapter 12

$\mathcal{T}$wo days after his meeting with Rich, Devon received the deed from their home in Virginia. His Dad wasted no time in ensuring his son had everything he needed. Devon had already gone over the household and church matters with Daria and other church members. It was time for him to turn himself in. There was no point in delaying the inevitable; the last thing he wanted was for the cops to come looking for him. After discussing additional arrangements with Daria, Devon called Joshua to pick her up; then he called Rich to pick him up.

"It's time," he said over the phone.

Rich wrapped up some things at the office and then went to the cottage to pick up his friend. Devon embraced his wife, pulling strength from her. Joshua and Stephanie were the first to arrive, but Daria insisted she not leave until Rich came. She wanted to spend every possible moment she could with her husband. Rich pulled up about thirty minutes after Joshua. It gave Joshua and Devon time to talk. Devon needed to make sure he was not overburdening his friend. He also wanted to ensure Joshua would do everything in his power to protect his wife. Lastly, he made Joshua promise that if he could not make bail for whatever reason, he would make sure

Daria went to her parent's house with the children. After their brotherly pow-wow, Devon walked back into the room with the ladies. They saw Rich's car pull into the driveway. Daria and Devon looked into each other's eyes one more time as he bent down to kiss her. Without another word being spoken, he walked out of the cottage and got into the car with Rich.

Daria asked Stephanie to call an emergency meeting at her house after they picked her up from the cottage. On the car ride, she couldn't bring herself to speak. Her mind was solely on her husband. During their conversation, Devon informed Joshua of his plans to turn himself in. He was not happy about this turn of events, but he understood. Daria also spent time alone with Stephanie to share what Rich suggested. Steph embraced her friend and ensured her Devon would come out on the right side of this situation.

It was almost five o'clock in the evening when they arrived at Joshua's and Stephanie's house. Steph asked the rest of the team, Deacon Maurice, Sister Treva, and Sister Angelique, to meet them at that time. Daria's head was throbbing with excruciating pain. So much so that Steph could see the pain in her eyes. She went to the kitchen to get Daria a glass of water and a sedative from her medical bag.

"Daria, you look like you need this. She held a small paper cup with half of a single pill in front of Daria. It's a mild sedative to help you relax and alleviate your headache."

"Will this put me to sleep? I can't sleep before sharing the details with everyone."

"No, it's only half a pill. When you are ready to sleep, I will give you a whole one to help you rest. I have a feeling you are going to need a little assistance if you are going to get any rest tonight."

"Thank you, Steph. I am going to need a lot of assistance. You are sweet for being so discerning."

"That's what friends are for!"

Daria went to the bathroom to splash a little water on her face so that her eyes would not look so puffy from the tears she had been crying. She lingered in front of her reflection in the mirror. Having been through tragedy before, God reminded her that she didn't look like what she'd been through. And she won't look like what she is going through now. Feeling reassured, she dried her hands and returned to the living room where the others were waiting.

"Lady Daria, are you okay?" Sister Treva asked as she walked into the room.

"To be honest, Sister Treva, not at all, but God just reminded me that He was still with us," Daria replied.

She turned to face the team that had been assembled. She thought she could stand before them to share what happened, but her legs were weak and limp like noodles. She quickly grabbed the back of the chair in front of her to avoid falling.

"Lady Daria, we are with you. Whatever has happened, you are not going through this alone," Sister Angelique reassured her. Although still holding on to the guilt about her conversation with the police, no one blamed her, and everyone seemed to understand. Even so, it didn't take away her sense of betrayal.

Daria offered a faint smile as she moved to sit in the beautiful tan and burgundy accent chair, which had previously buffered her fall. She glanced out the window facing the front yard for a few moments before addressing her team, church members, and, most importantly, friends. Then Daria began to recall the scene as though present when everything occurred. As she shared about the Hatchers, Nathan, and Gloria being eyewitnesses, her eyes surfed the room to see if the names were recognized by anyone. Seeing no notable signs, Daria told them what happened in the parking deck between Jocelyn Brandon and the assailant, who may or may not have killed her. Then she shared that Jocelyn was later found shot in the stomach.

"There's one more thing...after searching our home and Devon's office at the church, the police found a tissue and a half-empty water bottle in the garbage can in his office. It was from the items Jocelyn discarded before she left Devon's office. We all know now Jocelyn and Trini are one and the same. They also took his clothing and gun from our home. Thankfully, nothing was found to link him to the crime scene."

After repeating what Rich had shared with them, Daria quietly leaned back in her chair. The team sat stunned. Looking at everyone's face, Daria could see the expressions of concern, thoughts processing, and her least favorite, pity. The latter, of which she did not need.

She had to ask, "Do the names Nathan or Gloria Hatcher ring a bell?"

"I've met the Hatchers," Deacon Maurice spoke up. "I don't know them personally, but I was introduced to them by Lucas Jackson. They are his relatives."

Gasps echoed from the team. "Lucas?" Joshua spoke out in anger. "Do you think he had something to do with this? You know he has a vendetta against the Pastor...hell, for the whole church."

"Joshua!" Stephanie grabbed his arm.

"Sorry, not sorry! I don't mean to offend anyone with my language, but you know I don't hold my tongue," he responded sternly.

"No apologies necessary," Daria chimed in. "I am sure we all have some choice words we want to share right now. We don't know what he said while he was at the police station. Let's not go blaming anyone just yet. False accusations are what got Devon into this position. We don't want to stoop to that level."

"Rich informed us that because of eyewitnesses, camera footage, tissue, and DNA retrieved from the scene, there was enough for the police to issue a...," Daria could barely bring herself to say it, "a warrant for Devon's arrest."

"No!" Angelique and Deacon Maurice exclaimed.

"Unfortunately. Rich thought it best that, due to the circumstances, Devon should turn himself in," she paused.

"None of us like it, but Rich has a point. If there is a warrant out for his arrest, it is better that Pastor Devon goes to them like a man and not have the police searching for him. That would cause unnecessary attention," Joshua said, nodding his head.

"Yes, that's exactly what he said. He also mentioned a bail hearing in the morning, and we could need up to $50,000 to bail him out."

"We are happy to help cover the cost of his bail," Joshua said, looking over at his wife.

"Absolutely," Stephanie responded without hesitation.

"Count me in as well," Deacon Maurice added.

"I don't have very much, but I am happy to do what I can," shared Angelique.

"You guys are far too kind. We still have our house in Virginia to put up as collateral if it comes down to it."

Daria was touched by the offers and felt reassured of their commitment and for expressing their willingness to help. You can tell who your true friends are when money is involved.

"Wait, you said they have forensic evidence. I am assuming DNA or fingerprints?" asked Josh.

"From what I understand, it's both. The police found three separate sets of fingerprints," Daria replied.

"Ok, then, regardless of what they say they have on tape, the DNA and fingerprints will certainly prove his innocence."

"That's what we are hoping. The fact that Devon had an encounter with the victim before her death does not help his case. We have so much to pray about. This is all so overwhelming."

When Daria finished speaking, she again surfed the faces in the room. She could see the expressions of concern. After looking at Sister Treva, she saw something far different than ever before. Sister Treva was glowing. An actual real-life glow radiated from her body. It was as if her silent prayers had opened heaven's gates, and angels were ascending and descending at her command. The others followed Daria's gaze, and as they looked upon Sister Treva, they, too, saw the light illuminating their dear friend. Everyone fell silent. One by one, their silence became prayers, and prayers became worship, and worship led them directly into God's presence. The same place Sister Treva had ascended...the portal to heaven she had opened. The reverence they felt was not like any they had ever experienced before. It was an intimacy with the Father that most could only dream of having. They were standing, sitting, and kneeling in the very presence of God.

Though she was in awe of what was happening, somehow Daria was comforted by this visitation. She knew God would expose the works of darkness that tried to manifest in their lives. This level of worship was beyond intimate. It was as if each person in the room was one with God. They had a visitation with the Almighty One! It seemed like mere seconds, but in natural time, they were worshipping for well over an hour. As everyone began coming back from their worship experience, they could not speak, at least not in the English language. Their native vernacular failed them. It was another fifteen minutes before the room grew utterly silent again. As they looked at each other and then at Sister Treva, they realized they all had similar encounters with God. But it was clear to them that this was not Sister Treva's first.

The team sat in silence, still somewhat entranced. The fragrant scent of God's presence still lingered in the air; even the aromatic freshness ministered to them. Would they ever experience this level of worship again? Could their natural bodies endure such a high level of worship more than once? One thing was certain, they all felt a hunger for God they had never experienced before. It was an insatiable hunger that could only be filled by an Almighty God. Although the hour was late, no one wanted to leave the experience. They each had the same but different encounters with God. They could not wrap their heads around it, but they knew God had told them each something different...their worship was totally different, and yet it was the same.

Slowly they fully came to themselves and became aware of their surroundings. It was time for each of them to go to their respective homes. No more words needed to be spoken. God said everything which needed to be said. Out of respect for the anointing present, particularly over Daria and Sister Treva, everyone quietly got up and headed for the front door. It was as if God had given each of them a specific instruction, and they could not tarry. Sister Treva was the last to leave as she had a message for only Daria's ears. As she whispered the words to her, Daria gasped. Sister Treva told her she must remain silent until God instructed her to speak on it. Daria, still in disbelief, nodded to assure Sister Treva she would not say anything until the time was right.

As everyone was leaving, Daria excused herself and went upstairs to the guest bedroom. Steph previously readied the room for her with fresh linen and an oil burner, which filled the room with the scent of lavender. A glass of water and another small paper cup with a single pill sat on the nightstand. Daria changed into her night clothes, took the sedative with a few sips of water, and instantly drifted off to sleep. She could tell this sleep would be like none she had ever experienced.

Chapter 13

Chapter 3

$\mathcal{T}$he police station buzzed with activity. Uniformed detectives quickly rushed from one area to the next. Long lines of people waited to either see their loved ones or report a crime, and even more sat in seats in the small, cramped lobby. Several phone lines were ringing, inaudible conversations added to the noise in the room, and police sirens were heard in the distance.

"Never a dull moment," Devon thought as he walked up to a detective's desk with Attorney Harris. The wooden desk had an old bulky monitor sitting on it, as well as a crumb-covered keyboard with a greasy mouse sitting on a faded mousepad. The desk contained a folder, and papers were scattered randomly. There seemed to be no organization, but Devon assumed the Detective knew exactly where everything was.

"What brings you here, Rich," the police detective asked as he stood.

"Good evening, Greg," Attorney Harris reciprocated while initiating a handshake, "I need some discretion." The look on Attorney Harris' face let Detective Greg Bradley know this was serious.

Detective Bradley glanced over at Pastor Devon, and the nature of their visit was apparent. "Follow me," he instructed.

Detective Bradley led the two gentlemen into a room in the back of the station. The room had a cold, damp presence. There was not much light coming from the single light fixture that hung from the ceiling. On the left wall, there was a large mirror. Devon walked over to it and looked for a view of what was on the other side. He knew this was a two-way mirror, so they were clearly in one of the interrogation rooms. It was not the same room Devon was in when the police first questioned him. This one was a little larger but still as menacing.

"Have a seat, gentlemen," Detective Bradley gestured to the two chairs on the right side of an old desk. The desk had various scrapes in the wood finish, and when Devon put his hands on top, it wabbled.

"Greg...Detective Bradley," Attorney Harris corrected himself as he continued. "If you don't already know, this is Pastor Devon Royce."

"Yes, I recognize Pastor Royce." Devon and Detective Bradley exchanged a look and a slight head nod.

"Pastor Devon wants to fully cooperate with the investigation of the Brandon girl. He understands there is a warrant out for him, so he willingly came in to turn himself in."

"That's a noble gesture," assured Detective Bradley.

"Greg, this is a good man. I know he didn't do this. Please take care of him as best you can while he is here."

"I understand," Greg replied to his friend Rich. Turning to Pastor Devon, "I am sorry to have to do this, Pastor, but I have to officially place you under arrest."

"I understand," Pastor Devon replied.

"Please stand and put your hands behind your back, sir."

Pastor Devon complied as Detective Bradley Mirandized him. Still, he could not completely grasp what was happening, but he dared not seem combative. This may be a friend of Rich's, but he is still a police detective. Attorney Harris leaned over to Devon and whispered, "It's going to be okay. God will take care of you, and we will get you out of here as soon as possible."

Devon could not open his mouth to respond. Instead, he nodded at his attorney and his friend. Detective Bradley led Pastor Devon deeper into the police station. On the outside, the building did not look nearly as big as it was, or maybe the heaviness of each step Pastor Devon took made the journey seem like a scene from the movie *The Green Mile*. Detective Bradley stopped in front of a tall desk where another officer stood ready and somewhat eager to handle his intake process. He removed the handcuffs from Devon and went behind the desk to one of the computers. Shortly after, he walked over to the printer, grabbed a handful of papers, and placed them in a folder. Devon assumed that this was a part of his arrest jacket. Detective Bradley then had a conversation with the Officer at the desk.

"Sir, please remove all of your jewelry and empty everything out of your pockets," the officer said. She instinctively laid a plastic bag on the desk without looking up from her computer screen. Devon proceeded to remove all his jewelry, including his gold chain with the cross charm that his children gave him for his birthday. He slowly removed his wedding ring as thoughts of Daria flooded his mind. He proceeded to empty his pockets of his keys, wallet, and other miscellaneous items and then placed them all in the plastic bag.

"Stand with your back facing the wall," the Officer said as she looked up from her computer and pointed to a wall to her left. On the wall hung a dingy whiteboard with black horizontal lines. "A mug shot?" he thought to himself. A sick feeling arose deep in his gut. He felt humiliated as well as victimized. "Hold this," the officer commanded. "Turn to your left," the shudder from the camera clicked, and the light flashed. "Face forward," *snap*. "Turn to your right," *snap*.

Pastor Devon was escorted to a taller table where his fingers were dipped on an ink pad and pressed one by one on a special cardboard paper. First, his left, then his right, starting with his pinky and ending with his thumb on both hands. Devon was then read a list of instructions of do's and don'ts. Afterward, he was released back to Detective Bradley, who escorted him around the corner and into a holding cell.

"Pastor, this will be your room for the night. It is not the best accommodation, but it is not the worst either. I am on night shift, so I will come through as often as possible to check on you," he drew a little closer and whispered, "Officer Joyce's bark is worse than her bite. She takes her job seriously, but she is a good person." He opened the cell door, and as Devon walked in, he closed the door behind him. The sound of metal against metal made his heart drop. Devon turned to face Detective Bradley, "Rich and I are good friends. If he believes in you, so do I. I have heard you preach a few times; you seem to be the real deal. If your relationship with God is as strong as I think it is, you will be okay."

"I appreciate that," Devon was finally able to speak. "This seems unreal, but you are right; God has never failed me."

"Amen," Detective Bradley agreed before he walked away.

Devon looked around the jail cell. There was a low cot on the left wall of the cell with a thin, lumpy mattress and a single sheet covering it. At the foot of the cot was a pillow and blanket that was not much thicker than the sheet. In the far-right corner, there was a single commode emitting a pungent odor. The mere look of it made Devon wretch. He could understand how prisoners he met through the church prison ministry felt like caged animals. If this was the holding cell, he would hate to imagine how an actual prison cell felt. It was a feeling he did not care to experience.

After pacing back and forth for what seemed like an hour, he finally sat down on the cot. Though he was a pastor, he was a natural man facing the worst circumstances. He needed to get out of his head. He knew he could not face this without the help of the Lord. He really needed to wail out to God. Still, he decided against it for fear of prompting Officer Joyce to show him how serious she really was about her job. Instead, he sat on the metal cot with his head in his hands. He whispered a prayer, more like a plea, to God. He prayed in his natural tongue, and he prayed in his spiritual language. He declared and decreed, reminded God of His promises to him, and prayed boldly against the hand of the enemy on his life. If ever he needed God to step in, he most certainly needed Him now.

After he exhausted himself in prayer, he sat in silence, still in the same position. Now that he had poured his heart out to God, he waited for God to pour back into him. He heard God speak Deuteronomy 31:6, "Be strong and of a good courage, fear not, nor be afraid of them: for the Lord thy God, he it is that doth go with thee; he will not fail thee, nor forsake thee." Feeling the strong presence of God, even in jail, he laid down and rested. He knew he needed all his natural strength to face what would lie ahead.

Chapter 14

The following day, Daria woke to the smell of food and coffee wafting through the air. She initially looked around to check her surroundings, hoping yesterday's experience was a bad dream and she was home while Devon was downstairs cooking breakfast. As beautiful as the room was, it quickly became apparent it was not hers. She needed to face the fact this was not a dream. It was her current reality. She was reminded about the visitation which occurred the night before. She felt reassured God was working things out for her husband. Daria opened her suitcase to grab one of her favorite sweats and a T-shirt. After grabbing the neatly folded burgundy towel and wash cloth Stephanie left on a chair in her room, she walked down the hall to the guest bathroom. She brushed her teeth, put her hair in a bun, then headed downstairs to greet Stephanie and Joshua.

"Hi Daria, how did you sleep?" Stephanie asked as she placed a bowl of fruit on the dining room table.

"Surprisingly, I slept better than I expected," Daria responded as she took her seat at the table. "How long have you been up, and who will eat all this food?"

"I woke up a little early, so I decided to get breakfast going. Josh got a call from Rich this morning and ran out. He said they would return to the house, and I suspect that Deacon Maurice will be with them."

"Steph, I am so sorry we are disrupting your home with this insanity."

"Gurl, if you don't hush your face! With all the insanity you and Devon take on for all the people of the church, including Josh and me, it is only right we stand in the gap for you."

Daria smiled. "Thank you."

Josh and Rich were already coming through the front door as Daria finished a glass of juice. "Good morning, ladies," Rich said as he sat down his briefcase and headed into the dining room.

"Good morning," the ladies responded in unison.

"Rich, any news on Devon? Is he okay? What happened last night? I have been so worried."

"He is okay, Lady Daria. I made sure of it. One of my former army buddies works over there. I made sure he was the arresting officer. I assure you he is in good hands, all things considered."

Though this gave Daria a bit of reassurance, she still could not wrap her head around her husband needing an 'arresting officer.'

"Now, Daria, this is going to be a trying day for you, but you need every bit of your strength, so please make sure you eat and keep yourself hydrated. We need to be at the courthouse at 9 a.m. I am unsure where Devon's name is on the docket, so we need to get there as soon as they open the courthouse doors."

"I understand," she said as she picked at a little of the fruit she placed on her plate. On the other hand, Josh and Rich helped themselves to the feast Stephanie had laid out.

"Daria, at least have some eggs and toast. You are going to need something on your stomach." Without any arguments, Daria complied.

After breakfast, Daria went back upstairs to change into something more appropriate for court. As she began to descend the stairs, she heard Rich on what sounded like an official call. Hurrying to chime in on the conversation, she missed the last step causing her to lose balance, lunge forward, then faceplant onto the floor.

"Oh no! Daria, are you ok?" Stephanie yelled out.

"Oh, my goodness!" Joshua exclaimed as he ran to assist her in getting up and into a nearby chair.

Stephanie instinctively grabbed her medical bag and hurried to Daria's side to assess the damage. Luckily, there were only scrapes on the arm she fell on to brace the fall and a sprained right ankle. Stephanie applied an antibiotic ointment on the scratches, then applied an ankle brace after gauging the range of motion in Daria's ankle. She brought her a glass of water along with something for the pain.

"This was the last thing I needed," Daria shook her head as she awkwardly stood up to try to apply pressure to the hurt ankle. "I'm sorry, I heard Rich on the phone. I thought it could be about Devon's case. I guess I got a little overzealous."

Rich heard the commotion as he was getting off the call. "Young lady, I cannot have your husband see you all battered and bruised. He will think we did not take care of you as we promised."

"I know. I will take full responsibility for my clumsiness."

"You were right, though. The call was about Devon."

"What is it?" she asked as she limped towards Rich.

I am still trying to process it myself, but that was my contact at the police station. It appears they have gotten back the results of the forensic tests. Joshua and Stephanie joined Rich and Daria in the living room.

"Does this mean Devon will be released?" Joshua asked. All eyes turned back to Rich.

"That's the thing, so the fingerprints were not a match; however, the DNA was."

"What? How is that possible!" Daria exclaimed.

"I don't exactly know," Rich shrugged. "This is a new one on me unless there was more than one person involved."

"I don't care how many were involved. Devon's DNA could not possibly have been at the crime scene."

"Let's take a deep breath, this was just a preliminary finding, and my contact was sharing information that had not fully been vetted. Let's not panic. God is in control of the situation."

Daria tried her best not to have another outburst, but silent tears flowed. Stephanie handed her a tissue. "So, what does this mean," she asked as she tried to compose herself.

"Nothing has changed as far as today is concerned. We are still going to Devon's bail hearing, and we are still bringing him home. I was hoping for a lesser bail, but I am pretty sure the D.A. will push the highest amount possible, the $500,000 we discussed yesterday. The good part is we were already prepared for the worse case."

Daria sat in silence with her eyes closed. She whispered a prayer before opening her eyes. God seemed to surround her with His peace. "What are we waiting for? Devon is going to need to pull strength from all of us. Should we call Sister Treva and Deacon Maurice?"

"Deacon Maurice has already been alerted and will meet us there. He said when Sister Treva left here last night, she went straight to the courthouse. She has been praying and marching around that courthouse all night. From what I heard, she had gathered several other prayer warriors from our church and others. She had an army marching with her. It sounded like a scene straight out of the Bible...the walls of Jericho will certainly come tumbling down with Sister Treva on the case." Everyone laughed at the imagery. It was just like God to bring laughter to such a serious situation.

Chapter 15

As Daria sat in the courtroom, her ankle began to throb from her fall earlier in the day. To divert attention from her pain, she began surfing the faces in the courtroom. She saw people from all walks of life waiting for a judge's determination on the next course of their lives or those of their loved ones. Feeling a particular tug on her heart, her eyes landed on a woman in her mid-forties sitting with a younger woman on the opposite side of the courtroom a few seats back. Daria presumed them to be mother and daughter. Yet, with no intention of rudeness, she could not move her eyes away from them as she sensed something familiar. Although sure they were strangers, the young lady was mesmerizing and drawing Daria in. Suddenly, her daze was interrupted when the judge called her husband's name.

"Up next, the State against Devon Royce," Judge Singletary said, reading from the court docket. Moments later, Devon appeared in a doorway at the front left of the courtroom. Daria's stomach began to flutter, and her heartbeat accelerated. Devon's clumsiness walking with hands cuffed at his waist, and a long chain connected to shackled ankles caused him to look down at the restrictions. Once escorted to his place behind the podium, he looked up to search for familiar faces. He wore an oversized worn-out orange jumpsuit, white socks, and slip-on shoes, triggering him to shuffle his feet. Then he saw Daria seated beside Attorney Harris, and on her right was Stephanie, her anchor. Behind them were Deacon Maurice, Sister Angelique, and his buddy Joshua. Throughout the courtroom sat other familiar people and members of his congregation. Some he knew came to support him, while others were there to be gossipmongers. Nonetheless, his focus remained on his wife as much as possible.

Attorney Harris greeted Devon, and together they stood at a podium a few feet from the judge. The District Attorney stood at the right of the podium. Daria noticed an older woman sitting authoritatively in her seat a few rows behind him. The woman seemed agitated. Daria wondered if she was a relative of the deceased. Although she knew the woman would not receive her if approached after court, Daria made a mental note to pray for her and the family who had lost their beloved daughter. The judge read over the document in front of him and asked, "Devon Royce, how do you plead?"

"Your honor, my client pleads not guilty," Attorney Harris confidently replied.

"Very well," responded Judge Singletary. Turning to the D.A., "How do you want to proceed with bail?"

"Your Honor, we are asking bail to be set at $500,000."

"Your Honor," Attorney Harris interrupted, "my client is a respectable member of society. He is a Pastor in good standing at a local church and has never had so much as a parking ticket. I ask that he is released of his own recognizance."

"Come on, Your Honor!" the D.A. quickly interrupted with a mocking laugh. "Attorney Harris cannot be serious. This is a murder case, for God's sake." The crowd murmured among themselves.

Judge Singletary banged his gavel. "Order!" he demanded. "Save the theatrics for the actual trial," he warned. "Mr. Royce, I have reviewed your case, and I acknowledge the lack of any priors. If I release you, do you promise to appear back here on the date set by the court?"

Daria glanced back in the direction of the older woman, and she saw tears streaming from her eyes. She knew this woman must be related to Ms. Brandon. Maybe even her mother. She was clearly heartbroken Devon would be released. As much as it pained Daria to see the woman grieving, she felt a little offended that the woman wanted her husband to remain in jail.

"Yes sir, Your Honor," Devon responded.

"Judge Singleton...," the D.A. interrupted.

"Don't push me," he warned as he pointed his gavel to the D.A., then turned his attention back to Devon,

"You must have caught me on a good day. I do not believe you will be a flight risk. You must stay in North Carolina until your hearing. Do I make myself clear?"

"Yes Sir, Your Honor," Devon replied.

Judge Singletary briefly spoke to the court clerk and turned his attention back to Devon.

"Your court date is set for September 16th. Please convene with your attorney for further instructions. All of which must be adhered to," he said, pointing his gavel at Devon and raising one eyebrow. "Don't take my kindness for weakness. If you are brought back with so much as a jay-walking ticket, I will not be so nice."

"Thank you, Your Honor!" Devon and Attorney Harris both echoed. Attorney Harris grabbed the file in front of him, whispered in Devon's ear, and turned and winked at Daria. Devon also turned to Daria and mouthed, "I love you!"

She responded the same, positioning her hands on her chest in a heart-shaped formation. Devon was escorted out of the same doorway he entered. Attorney Harris walked down the aisle, signaling Daria and the others to follow him out of the courtroom. They grabbed their things and quickly exited. Attorney Harris escorted them into an empty room not far from the courtroom they left.

Daria noticed the older woman, who appeared to be related to Ms. Brandon, rush past them and gave her a piercing gaze. Before Daria could decide whether to say anything, the woman was out of sight. Daria knew it wasn't wise to look for her.

"Angelique, can you run and get Sister Treva?" Daria asked.

"Of course," Angelique responded. But as she was about to descend the stairs, she saw Sister Treva coming up.

"Sister Treva, I was just coming to get you."

"I know; thought I would save you a few steps," Sister Treva replied.

"How did she know?" thought Angelique, but then she remembered the encounter the night before and understood.

"What just happened, Rich?" Daria asked as Sister Treva and Angelique entered the room.

"God's favor," responded Sister Treva. She caught Daria's eye and gave her a wink. Daria did not question it, assuming it was just a show of affection.

"Indeed, it was God's favor. So, as you heard, Pastor Devon is getting released of his own recognizance. This means you do not have to put up any bail money. He will essentially sign some documents and be released."

"I can't believe it!" Daria exclaimed.

"If I'm being honest, I don't believe it either. The D.A. was right; this is a murder investigation. It is rare for someone accused of murder to get released without posting bail. Maybe because the judge knew the evidence was circumstantial. Nevertheless, God has truly favored Pastor Devon on this one."

Resounding amens echoed through the room. "So, how long before Devon gets released?" Joshua asked.

"Unfortunately, it is a slow process; it may take a couple of hours. As difficult as it may be, we must be patient. I am grateful we can celebrate Pastor Devon's release but let's not get too far ahead of ourselves. We still have more hurdles to jump. We may have won this battle, but we still have a war to fight. Pastor Devon is not out of the woods yet; he is still accused of murder, and we still must mount his defense."

"One mountain at a time," Sister Treva chimed in.

"Sister Treva, thank you so much for all your prayers and support. I don't know how you organized your marching army so quickly, but I recognize God heard you all, and His response was to release my husband."

"I am only executing God's plan. This may not be over. God knows the end from the beginning, and all things work together for His good."

"Amen," everyone sang out in unison.

"Lady Daria, since we have a little time before our dear pastor is released, why don't we sit in the courtroom. I think there may be one more case you need to witness," Sister Treva took Daria by the arm and gave another wink. This time Daria knew there was more behind the wink. Without question, she walked back into the courtroom with Sister Treva. The others went outside. Daria and Sister Treva sat near the back of the courtroom this time. On the same side as before but in the very back.

Again, Daria found herself surfing the room until her eyes laid upon the older woman and her daughter. She saw them react when the judge called the next defendant, Lawrence Douglas. As the defendant made his way to the podium to stand beside his attorney, Daria gasped. Initially, it did not sink in, but she realized the defendant was someone she once called her uncle. The defendant was the same man who sexually assaulted her as a teen. She watched as the young lady tensed up, and the mother lovingly placed her arm around her daughter. Without hearing the charges, Daria already knew what had happened. She looked at Sister Treva and back at the mother and daughter.

"Sister Treva, how did you know? I never told you."

"God reveals what He needs to reveal when He needs to reveal it. Do you remember what I whispered in your ear?" Sister Treva asked.

"Yes, I remember."

"God knows His business. He said you had a ministry waiting for you in that courthouse."

"Yes, I remember. Those were your exact words."

"But He also said you would be Harriet Tubman for other young ladies who shared the same heartbreaking experience as you. God said He had to position you in this place at this time so you could do what He needed you to do."

The ladies continued to stay seated until the conversation about his bail was over. Daria was relieved to hear he was not given bail because he was a repeat offender. Her stomach churned at the mere thought of this man hurting any other woman. She was healed from what happened to her, but it took a lot of time and patience. Now she knew she had to reach out to this young lady to help her walk through her own healing.

When the young lady and her mother left the courtroom, Daria followed behind them. "Excuse me," she said as she approached the two women.

A little startled, they both halted their conversation and turned toward Daria.

"I am so sorry to bother you. My name is Daria, my husband and I are over Faith Hope and Love Church," she said as she handed them a card.

"We have heard of it," the mother responded.

"I am so sorry about what you have gone through," Daria said, looking at the young lady.

"I'm sorry, Mrs. Daria. How do you know what either of us has gone through?" the mother interrupted.

"Because I know Lawrence Douglas, and because he did the same thing to me when I was younger."

The two ladies looked at each other stunned. "You know Larry?" the mother asked.

"Yes, I used to call him Uncle Larry. He wasn't really an uncle, but he was supposedly a good friend of my father. My Dad did not know what happened to me until well after it happened."

"I'm so sorry," the mother said as she softened her expression.

"I would love to sit down and talk with you both whenever you have some time. While sitting there listening, God told me I needed to minister to the young women who experienced the same hurt I had suffered. I don't mean to be nosey, and I am not trying to assert myself in your business, but if you want to talk to someone who knows what you have been through, please call me."

"Thank you," the young lady responded.

"I am Fiona, and this is my daughter Sharee," the eldest lady offered her hand as she introduced herself and her daughter.

"Pleased to meet both of you," Daria responded, accepting the handshake. "I look forward to hearing from you both." With that, Daria turned and walked to where Sister Treva was standing.

"Well done," Sister Treva said as Daria approached.

"Do you think she will reach out?"

"I know she will. Now let's get you out of here and back with your husband," she chuckled as she grabbed Daria's arm and walked towards the elevator. Sister Treva was intense but also funny when she wanted to be. Her heart was bigger than anyone Daria had ever met. She was grateful Sister Treva was in her life. She made her a better person.

Chapter 16

$\mathcal{J}$oshua and Stephanie dropped Devon off at home and told him they would be back after running a few errands. He walked through the doors feeling immense gratitude and a new appreciation for what he had and where he lived. Even though the jail stent was only one night, it was one of the longest, scariest, and most stressful nights of his life.

"Baby, I am so sorry to put you through all of this," he turned to face Daria.

"Shhh...," she said with her index finger to her pursed lips. "Just hold me."

"Gladly!" Devon responded, wrapping his arms around the love of his life. They stood in the middle of the living room for several minutes in a warm and loving embrace until the doorbell interrupted them. There were still reporters out front, but they dare not enter their property or have the audacity to ring their doorbell. Devon looked through the peephole in the door before opening it.

"Now, are you going to tell me what happened to your ankle?" Devon asked as he opened the front door.

"Let's just say I keep falling for you," she said with a hearty laugh.

"Good to see you back in your environment," Joshua said as he and Stephanie entered. Although the Royces were happy to be back home and longed for their own bed, everyone pleaded with them to not stay in their home until this mess was resolved. The invitation to stay at the cottage was still on the table. Although Daria and Devon knew it was for the best, they were not happy about it. But if they must leave their home, they could not think of a better place to be than at the Evans' beautiful oasis.

"Let me run upstairs and shower," Devon said as he ascended the stairs.

"I guess I better get us some more clothes," Daria added. "Please help yourselves to something to drink. We will be back down shortly."

Stephanie and Joshua knew their way around the Royce home. Joshua went to the refrigerator to grab two bottles of water for himself and his better half. They sat playfully flirting with each other while waiting on Daria and Devon. They had been married for ten years and still enjoyed each other's company. It was evident in how they looked at each other. They were best friends as well as lovers. The two sat on the sofa giggling when Daria hobbled back down the stairs, still favoring her injured ankle. She always loved the chemistry between the two love birds.

"You two can't keep your hands off each other," Daria teased as she hopped to a chair positioned at the bottom of the stairs. Her ankle hurt even more than before.

"After all we have been through, I wouldn't want to," Stephanie responded as she assisted her friend. "Daria, you really need to elevate this ankle. I also have a bottle of water and some pain pills to lessen the discomfort and swelling."

"I will, I promise," she assured her friend, taking the medicine and the water. "Devon shouldn't be too much longer. Josh, have you heard from Rich since leaving the courthouse?"

"He told me he had something to take care of, but he would meet us back at the house a little later."

"Ok, I am excited to have Devon back home, but I know we are still facing an uphill battle."

"True, but you have some great people in your corner fighting with everything they've got. I know it is easier said than done but don't let this stress you too badly. Focus on Devon being home; the rest will work itself out."

When Devon came down the stairs, the two couples left. This time Devon drove his car so he could be mobile while trying to sort everything out. They decided to stop for lunch while out and went to a local family-owned restaurant they often frequented. The restaurant was only twenty minutes away. Upon entering the restaurant and walking up to the counter to order, they noticed glances and whispers from the onlookers. Consequently, they decided not to give energy to the gossipers. The restaurant owners escorted them to a separate room from the lunch crowd. No need for them to feel like fish in an aquarium while they tried to enjoy their dining experience.

"Pastor Devon, you know we support you. Please let us know if you and your beautiful bride need anything," the couple said before retreating to the kitchen.

As they waited for their food to arrive, Joshua began to speak. "Stephanie, Lady Daria, do you remember the visitation last night?"

"Visitation, what visitation?" Devon queried.

"How could we forget," Stephanie responded.

Daria turned to her husband, "It was something I have never experienced before. Sister Treva seemed to have opened the very gates of heaven. She was glowing, and angels were ascending and descending all around her."

"Daria, what are you talking about?" Devon chuckled, but as he looked at the faces around the table, he saw maybe his wife was not exaggerating.

"She's not kidding," Josh confirmed. "Man, all I know is one minute I was sitting in our living room, and the next I was standing at the very feet of God. He was an overwhelming presence draped in a long camouflage robe; unlike anything I had ever seen. He spoke in army lingo with great power and authority. I could understand His commands, but I don't know if any of the rest of you could follow."

"No, wait..." Stephanie interrupted, shaking her head. "He was wearing a beautiful purple robe that trailed far behind him; he was so gentle and beautiful to look upon. He spoke in a soft voice that was soothing to my soul. Although His presence was commanding, He certainly was not barking military commands."

"Did we all have different encounters?" Daria inquired. "My image of God had a host of angels surrounding Him. He wore a gold robe, and before Him, a bountiful feast was prepared. There was a beautiful ivory table with more food than I had ever seen. He sat right beside me and spoke in poetic verse. He spoke to me in a very clear and direct way giving me comfort and letting me know there was nothing too hard for Him, not even this."

The trio looked at one another with confused gazes. "How could it be? We all had the same experience but vastly different?" Josh asked. As harmonious as it felt, they discovered each encounter was unique. Even the aroma which lingered after was described differently. The descriptions of God were all over the place.

The others grew silent. It made Devon stop and think. Finally, Devon spoke up. "I wasn't there, but it sounds to me that God truly is everything to everyone. None of you had the exact same needs, so God had to present Himself to each one of you the way you needed to encounter him. What an amazing revelation!"

Their food arrived soon after, and the party of four did not hesitate to indulge in the feast before them. After consuming a good portion of food, silence passed, and faces and bellies were satisfied, they enjoyed each other's company. They shared details about their God encounters as well as other things that happened since they last saw Devon. The merriment was a much-needed relief from the strategy sessions they had been having over the last week. An hour passed before Devon's phone rang; it was Rich.

"Yes, we just wrapped up lunch. We will meet you there," Devon said, ending the call. He shared Rich needed to see them. Without hesitation, he left a generous tip on the table, and the foursome headed for the door.

They arrived at the cottage just as Rich was pulling up. Everyone said their pleasantries as they entered the cottage and seated themselves in the living room.

"Let's get to it," Rich began as he opened his briefcase. "This is what we know. There is an eyewitness account and camera footage. Ms. Brandon was still alive when she was placed into her car. The fingerprints did not match Devon's; however, the DNA was his."

"Yes, we know all of that, but what does it mean?" asked Devon.

"It means the D.A. does not have enough evidence to build a solid case. They reached out to me to make a plea deal."

"Plea deal? Absolutely not. I did not commit this crime. I had nothing to do with it. If we take a plea deal, it is as if I am confessing to the murder."

"I agree with you, Devon. I just had to present it to you."

"So, what do we do?" asked Daria.

"I am working on another angle; my researchers are following up on a lead. I don't want to get into details right now because I don't want to give false hope. But I will say that we can clear you, Devon. Though the Hatchers place the assailant at the parking garage, no one can put this assailant at the scene of the actual murder. The best they can do is charge you for a misdemeanor. If they somehow could prove at least that, you would get off on probation and must attend an anger management class. Now before any of you say anything...I know Devon did not do it. I am simply saying even the worst-case scenario is nowhere near as bad as it was at the beginning of this."

"I hear you, Rich. So, what now?"

"Now you spend time with your wife and your friends and let my team do what they do. We will get to the bottom of this and clear your name."

"Thank you, Rich," Daria said. "I know you are fighting for us. We cannot ask for anything more."

Daria excused herself from the meeting when her phone rang. It was her father-in-law. She stepped out on the back patio to answer the call.

"Hello," the senior Pastor Royce began.

"Hi, Daddy Royce," Daria greeted her father-in-law.

"Please tell me you have good news for me."

"Yes, Dad. Devon was released of his own recognizance. We do not have to put the house up for bail."

"Praise Jesus!" Pastor Royce chimed.

"Amen," Daria agreed.

"So, what next? Are they still trying to say he has something to do with killing this poor woman?"

"Unfortunately, Dad."

"Oh wow! When does he get out?"

"He is out now. Would you like to speak with him?"

"Yes, please," Daria could hear the relief in his voice.

"Devon," Daria said as she poked her head through the door. "Daddy Royce is on the line."

Devon excused himself and traded places with Daria on the patio as she handed him her phone. Devon briefed his father on all that happened. After Pastor Royce prayed for his son, the two ended their phone conversation, and Devon rejoined the group.

It was getting later in the day, and Devon and Daria were both tired. The team dispersed to give them a chance to share some quality time. It was a moment the couple needed. They sat on the loveseat with smooth jazz playing. They reminisced about the jazz restaurant they visited on their first date. They laughed at the memories as they enjoyed each other's company until they drifted off to sleep.

Chapter 17

$\mathcal{A}$ few days passed before Devon heard any real news on the case. He was still addressing church business to keep things as normal as possible. To maintain a low profile, everything was executed through phone calls or Zoom, and some responsibilities were delegated to the faithful staff at the church. Although he liked to be a hands-on pastor, he was surrounded by an awesome team of people who could fill in seamlessly.

Daria spent her time making sure her husband's needs were met. She loved being Devon Royce's wife. When he was happy, she was happy. While sitting on the deck enjoying the peaceful sounds of nature, she received a call from Sharee asking to meet. Daria told her husband about the encounter with Sharee at his bail hearing. After all these years, Larry, Lawrence Douglas, was still up to his same demented games, robbing young ladies of their purity. Denying them their power...dismissing their 'no.' Devon encouraged Daria to meet Sharee and assured her he would be fine. He told her not to get into any trouble. The two laughed, considering the situation he had already found himself in. Devon did not have to look for trouble; it somehow found its way to him.

Daria sat at one of the empty tables along the beautiful brick-layered fountain on College Street in Uptown Charlotte. The setting was breathtaking. Various fountains seemed to take turns dancing to their own rhythm as they joyfully spewed water higher, lower, then higher again. It was as if they were dancing to their own beat. The sun glistened on the water streaming in the air, making it appear to sparkle. Although Daria often visited the Uptown area, she seldom had a chance to just sit and admire the view. She was enjoying the glorious warm summer day and picked the perfect spot for people-watching, a favorite pastime. It was something about God's human creation that fascinated her. Everyone was so different yet had many of the exact wants and needs. She smiled and reminisced about her beautiful family as a husband, wife, and two children took pictures by one of the statues nearby. With everything going on, she finally realized how much she missed her children. Sure, they had Zoom calls twice a day, but it was nothing like being with them, listening to giggles, and watching their shenanigans firsthand.

She was happy when Sharee suggested they meet near her job. Sharee worked in a high-rise building along College Street. It was more convenient for her to meet Daria Uptown during lunch break rather than juggle busy schedules after work. Sharee was a new mother, a product of Larry's sexual assault. It was difficult for her to juggle working and being a mom. Daria admired her as she knew all too well what she was going through. She, too, had been impregnated by Larry but did not birth his child. Daria wanted to do whatever was within her power to help this young lady as much as she could.

As she continued to look around, Sharee came out of one of the tall buildings that made up the skyline of Uptown. She handed Daria a fresh iced mocha latte as they greeted one another. Sharee said she worked in a coffee shop in one of the buildings. Daria offered to buy her lunch, but she didn't have much of an appetite and politely declined. The ladies sat and talked for most of Sharee's lunch period. They shared how each knew Larry, the molester, and what made each victim regain control. For Sharee, it was much sooner than it was for Daria. Sharee's strength and lack of fear to stand up for herself really impressed Daria. Sharee promised she would soon visit Faith Hope and Love Church on a Sunday. The two talked a bit longer and then parted ways as it was time for Sharee to return to work.

After pondering their conversation a little longer, Daria took a few more sips of the iced coffee, pushed her chair back under the table, and fumbled in her purse for car keys. As she walked towards the parking garage, she looked to her left and was pleasantly surprised. There was her husband walking on the other side of the street. "What is he doing Uptown?" she mumbled. She crossed over to meet him; maybe they could grab a late lunch. As she drew closer, she was more stunned than surprised. The man she saw was not her husband, but he looked so much like him! "How could that be?" She watched him as he entered one of the bars on the strip. She quickly grabbed her phone and called her husband.

Impatiently pacing awaiting him to answer, she finally heard his voice, "Devon! Where are you?"

"I'm at the cottage. What's wrong? Are you okay?" he asked, confused by her tone.

"You are not going to believe this."

"What is it, Daria? What's wrong?"

"I was on my way to the car, and I saw someone I thought was you from a distance, but the closer I got to him, I knew it wasn't you. But Devon... he looked just like you!"

"Baby, that's impossible."

"Wait, let me see if I can get a picture. He's coming out of the building." Daria positioned her phone to get a good picture of this familiar stranger. She took a few pictures, then thought the stranger saw her snapping him, so she moved the phone to her side. Once she saw he was no longer fixed on her, she sent the pictures to her husband.

"Are you still there? Did you get them?" she asked, reeling from the rush of playing detective and almost getting caught.

"Oh my God! There is no way...it can't be!" Devon exclaimed. "Baby, I need to make a phone call."

"Okay, I am on my way back. Devon, this could be the man the couple saw. Surely anyone could have mistaken him to be you if he could fool me from a distance. OMG, we have proof it was not you!" excitement exuded as she spoke.

"Yes, hurry back but be careful. Remember, this could be the assailant. He could be dangerous."

"I know. I was discreet when I took the pictures. He's walking in the opposite direction now. See you in a few."

When Daria arrived back at the cottage, she noticed several cars outside. Rich, Josh, and Deacon Maurice were gathered on the back patio. Daria walked through the house and out the back door to be with her husband and find out what was happening.

"Daria," Devon started. "Do you remember me telling you I had a twin brother who was abducted when we were young? He couldn't have been any more than six years old."

"Yes, you guys were in Mexico, right? You said there was a marketplace your family visited often. He stopped to look at something at the market, but you guys didn't notice him stopping. Before any of you realized what happened, he was gone." Even the thought of a child being abducted made Daria wince and miss her own babies even more.

"What if..."

"Devon, it couldn't be, could it?"

217

"It certainly is an extraordinary story," Rich chimed in. "But it could prove why the DNA matched but not the fingerprints. Identical twins share the same DNA, but their fingerprints are unique."

"*OMG!* So maybe Trini slept with Donté but thought it was Devon. I mean, his billboard is posted off the highway near the church. Maybe, just maybe, she thought they were one and the same. I mean, that's the only thing that makes sense! She accused Devon of sleeping with her, but it really was Donte!" Daria exclaimed.

"Before we get too wound up, we need to find this person again. My research team is looking into the theory of the suspect being related to you. I think now is the time to share this theory with my buddy at the station. If we can find this mystery person, we can clear everything up and get the charges against you dropped."

Daria turned to Devon, "Baby, what will this mean for your family? You all thought he was dead."

"I don't know," he said with uncertainty. "I am still trying to wrap my mind around the possibility of Donté being alive after all this time."

"I will keep you guys posted as soon as I hear anything," Rich said as he quickly headed to the front door. He had to get a jump on this new information right away. Deacon Maurice left as well.

Joshua, however, decided to stay for a bit longer, just in case his friend needed him. He went outside to work around the cottage and process what was happening rather than intrude or say anything. Nothing really needed to be done; Joshua just wanted to keep busy and watch over his friend. Although Devon could not acknowledge him because of all the noise in his head, he knew Joshua was there and appreciated him even more.

Stephanie called her husband when she got off work, and Joshua told her what had happened.

"*OMG!*" she exclaimed. "Now it makes sense...a twin brother...*WOW!*"

"I will be home as soon as I can. I must make sure Devon is okay before I leave. I mean, this is a lot to absorb."

Devon paced back and forth, back and forth, and tried desperately to process what was happening before he called his parents. What would they say when they learned that Donté, his brother, could be alive? Would he remember them? Where has he been? What happened to him? What did he go through? Who raised him? What did he do to this young lady? So many thoughts raced through his mind. He could not silence the questions.

Daria could see her husband's turmoil, and she wanted so much to help, but there was not much she could do. She had to let him process all of this in his own way, in his own time. She knew he would have a million questions for God, and they would even have heated conversations. But once he got it all out, he could address it, and God would lead him in the right direction. As helpless as she felt, she was grateful Joshua stuck around after everyone else left. Sometimes men just need the presence of other men. She understood that.

Chapter 18

Chapter 8

$\mathcal{D}$onté Smith was an identical replica of his brother Pastor Devon Royce. Looking at the pictures Daria had taken of him the previous day; Devon was still in shock his brother was in Charlotte. In all those years, he was still alive!

Devon waited until Attorney Harris could confirm the person Daria saw was indeed his abducted brother. He did not want to promote false hope in his parents. Even if this was his brother, Devon needed to determine his involvement in Ms. Jocelyn Brandon's murder. He could not bear to give them news their son was alive and tell them he had committed such a heinous act.

Attorney Harris had a suspicion long before Daria's revelation that Devon may have a sibling out there. It was the only way to explain the DNA match but not the fingerprints. He had his paralegal make some calls to find out the history of Devon's parents, Pastor and Mrs. Jonathon Royce. He did not know what would be unearthed; however, Daria's discovery solidified his suspicion. He did not want to say anything to Devon until he had proof, as he did not want to bring upheaval to his family. They were already going through enough as it was. Devon's brother had been abducted and presumed dead as the years passed. The paralegal found an address in Concord, North Carolina, for Mr. Donté Smith. His last name was apparently changed by his abductor.

Or maybe he could not remember his last name since he was so young; therefore, he decided to adopt the last name, Smith. They forwarded this information and their suspicion to Detective Bradley, who investigated after his shift.

Detective Bradley surveilled Donté's home until he was confident he should bring his sergeant up to speed. Surprised by this new revelation, the sergeant made sure he followed proper protocol to get a search warrant. Several Detectives went to Donté Smith's house to search it after obtaining a warrant signifying probable cause. Detective Bradley rang the doorbell, followed by knocking on the door. Donté opened the door.

"Mr. Smith," Detective Bradley spoke as he flashed his badge. "We have a warrant to search your premises."

"Search my premises? For what? What did I do?" Donté inquired, startled by this interruption.

"We have reason to believe you were involved in the murder of Ms. Jocelyn Brandon," Bradley continued as he pushed his way past Donté. The other Detectives followed suit.

"Jocelyn Brandon?" I don't know anyone by that name. Man, what is this about?"

"You may know her as 'Trini.'

"What! Trini is dead? Man, I didn't even know her like that. I slept with her once or twice, but I didn't know her to know her and certainly had no reason to kill her!"

While the policemen were trampling through his home, Donté called legal aid. He knew whatever was going on it was best he prepared himself by speaking with an attorney. Forty minutes passed before the policemen convened back in Donté's living room. They reported to Detective Bradley they did not find a weapon or anything else that could be used against Donté.

"A weapon? Can someone please tell me what is going on?" Donté insisted.

Detective Bradley motioned the other police detectives to leave the home while he sat down with Donté. "Mr. Smith, you mentioned you did indeed know, Jocelyn; I'm sorry, Trini Brandon, correct?"

"Yes, I met her at a club a couple of months ago. We were vibing, and one thing led to another. I saw her again once or twice, but then I didn't hear anything else from her. I knew she had a man, so I figured she must have gotten caught up."

"Can you tell me where you were last Thursday at approximately 10 p.m.?"

Donté sat back in his chair to think about his whereabouts that day. As he was thinking, it dawned on him what must have happened. "Detective, I was in Uptown Charlotte that night. I met some friends earlier in the evening, left them, and headed back to my car to go home. On my way to my car, I got a call from Trini. She must have seen me at the bar. It's where we first met. She asked me to meet her in the garage because she had something to tell me."

"Was your car in the Tryon Street parking garage, sir?"

"Yes, it was. I think I see where this is going. I did not meet with her right away. I went to my car first to make a call. Man, I figured if she could ghost me, I could take my time meeting up with her. I ended my call abruptly because I heard a man and woman arguing a few spots up from me. Typically, I would ignore it because people do what they do. But this particular night, I heard the young lady screaming and then nothing."

"Go on," Detective Bradley beckoned.

"Well, I got out of my car to see what happened. I saw the young lady on the ground, it was Trini! She was unconscious, and a man was getting up from beside her. I figured he was her man. When I yelled out, the man ducked around the front of a few other cars and disappeared from sight. I kneeled beside Trini; I could tell she was still alive but unconscious. I called 911 but was put on hold. So, I got her up and put her in the backseat of her car. Then I got her keys out of her purse so I could drive her to the hospital. She was beginning to come to, and I could hear her mumbling something about a baby. She seemed delirious. I kept saying, 'Trini, it's me, Donté. Then she kept asking me why I played her at the church. Man, I had no idea what she was talking about because I don't do churches."

"Interesting," Bradley chimed in once more.

"As I was driving, another car came out of nowhere and forced us off the road. I ended up running into a tree. My head hit the steering wheel, and I was unconscious. When I came to, I looked around for Trini, but she was no longer in the backseat. I got out of the car, and that's when I saw her. She was only a few feet from the car. I went over to her, and when I got closer, I saw blood. There was so much blood."

"So, are you saying she was thrown from the car?"

"No...I don't know. What I do know is blood was streaming everywhere. When I pushed her on her back, her hands fell limp, and I could see blood gushing from her stomach." Donté had to stop for a minute to collect himself as he recalled the gruesome sight. Suddenly, it was as if a light bulb had turned on. Was she calling him to the garage to tell him she was pregnant with his baby? This was all too much for him to handle.

"Did you see anyone else? Maybe the driver of the car?"

"I couldn't see because it all happened so fast. When I came to from the accident, no one else was around. The car that hit us was gone. I can only assume it was her guy! It had to be. I heard them arguing over a baby. Maybe he was angry because she may be pregnant by another man. I just don't know. I can't believe she was even pregnant. The baby...did dude kill my baby?"

"Let's not jump to conclusions, Mr. Smith," Brandon attempted to keep Donté calm. So, did you call 911 after the accident?"

"No, they wouldn't answer me when I first found her, so I didn't think to call them again. Plus, I panicked. There was no way I could explain any of this. Especially if the baby really was mine. I couldn't explain why I had her car and why she had all the bruises on her and a gunshot to her stomach. All I wanted to do was get her to a hospital. I was trying to be a good Samaritan. Man, I panicked. I can't get caught up in the system. Had I stuck around, I would have been arrested, tried, and convicted before the handcuffs were locked around my wrists. All in the blink of an eye."

Detective Bradley sat quietly, trying to absorb the story he had just heard. Although Donté's account did fill in some of the holes, the fact remained he was the last person to see this woman alive.

"Look, I know it was wrong not to report it, but like I said, I panicked. I have enough problems of my own. I no longer needed to associate myself with whatever was going on with her."

"The man you saw her arguing with, can you describe him?"

"I guess he was a White man or maybe a Latino, about five foot seven and medium build. He ran before I could get a good look at him. He had on a hoodie, so I couldn't see his hair color, but the left sleeve of his hoodie was pushed up, and I could see a tattoo. The tattoo was the area code 704 with the four dripping like it was melting or something."

"Do you remember what else he was wearing? What color was the hoodie?"

"The hoodie was light blue, and he wore dark blue jeans or maybe black. That's really all I can remember about him."

"Would you be willing to come down to the station so we can get your official statement?"

"Yes, anything to get me out of this mess."

"By the way, do you know Pastor Devon Royce?"

Donté sat quietly for a moment. Detective Bradley could tell something was registering with him. He waited patiently for Donté to respond. It was evident a connection was being made. "Royce...Royce...OMG! I had a brother named Devon, Devon Royce, my twin brother. I haven't seen him since we were kids. Something happened that separated me from my family. Why do you ask?"

"He is the Pastor of a local church here in Charlotte."

After a long pause, he responded, "The billboard! Man, the billboard. It's beginning to make sense. Trini told me she had seen my picture on a billboard. I figured she had me mistaken for someone else, but she was so fine I went with it. I'm a single man...anything to get in good, know what I'm saying? She would say, 'you are that guy on the billboard off 77. I am in the presence of a celebrity.' Man, my brother is a pastor? Here? Wow! I guess that tracks. Sounds like he took after his father. Well, our father..."

"Do you mind if I ask what happened to separate you from your family?"

"I was so young. I remember being at an outdoor market looking at some toys. When I turned around, my family was gone. A man came up behind me and bought me the toy he noticed me admiring in front of one of the vendor stands. He told me he would help me find my parents, but he led me to his car instead. From there, he told me he talked to my parents over the phone, and they said they could no longer afford to take care of my brother and me, so he offered to take care of me."

"Oh no, that's horrible. Did he hurt you?"

"No. Well...at least not at first," Donté's words trailed off.

"Where is this man now?"

"He died about five years ago. He was the only father I remember. Although he did some real messed up stuff to me, at least he tried to care for me as best he could. A lot more than I can say about my real family. As a child, I could not understand what was happening. Now that I know I was abducted, I never understood why my family didn't work harder to find me.

Detective Bradley knew not to push things any further. "I don't know much about your family, but I have met your brother. From what I can tell, there is a lot of love in his heart. I am sure they didn't just give up, but that's not for me to say. But look, I have to be honest with you. Based on what you have shared, I must place you under arrest. Even if you did not commit the murder of Ms. Brandon, you did tamper with the original crime scene, and you left the scene of a crime."

"I know it was wrong; I just didn't know what to do. I've been in lock up before, and I didn't want to have to go through it again. But I get it. Do what you gotta do. I do have to know one thing, was the baby really mine?"

"No, we confirmed the DNA under Ms. Brandon's fingernails, and the DNA from the baby was a match. Whoever murdered her was the father of the baby."

Donté hung his head.

Chapter 19

*A*ll charges have been dropped," an elated Attorney Rich Harris said as he walked through the front door of the cottage. Everyone had already gathered when they received a call from Rich's office. Shouts of joy and thanksgiving filled the room.

"I don't know how to thank you," a grateful Pastor Devon said as he embraced his friend.

"Pastor, with all you have gotten my family and me through, this was the least I could do for you," Rich replied.

After the excitement and celebration died down, Daria turned to Rich. "So, was Donté the one who killed that poor woman?"

"No, the police were able to corroborate his story. He really was trying to help the young lady. Although he did not go about things the right way and failed to report what happened, he acted with good intent. He still must serve jail time for moving Ms. Brandon and not reporting the crime, but he should be out in eighteen months. I will work with him to see if we can get it reduced."

"Praise God! Thank you for looking out for him! Man, thank you for everything you have done for me. I couldn't have gotten out of this mess without you!" Devon chimed in, relieved. "Did they find the man that did this to her?"

"Not yet, but they are close. We have the suspect's name, and it was confirmed that he was the father of her baby. The tattoo Donté saw on the assailant's left arm is a part of a cult affiliation. Not many people walk around with the type of tattoo Donté described."

"What about Ms. Brandon's family?" Daria thought back to the day at the courthouse.

"They simply want justice for their daughter."

"Is there any way we can invite them to the church? We have been praying for them since this all began, but I would love to speak with them and let them know we're standing with them.

"So many lives have been altered by this tragedy. I know God is up to something...there has to be glory after this!" Devon insisted, agreeing with his wife.

"I don't know if that's possible, but I will see what I can do. No promises. Even though you and Donté aren't responsible, I don't know how receptive they will be."

"I understand."

"Well, my work here is done. I am glad we cleared the good Pastor, and I pray you can be reunited with your brother."

"Thank you, I will call my parents so we can all be together when we reunite with him. If I'm being honest, I don't know how to begin this healing process."

"I spoke with Donté briefly; he, like you, has a lot of questions as well as a lot of pain. He mentioned to Detective Bradley how he felt abandoned. He said he couldn't understand why your family didn't try harder to find him. But he is open to meeting you and your family once he is released. I would say to be patient with him and let the Lord lead you."

Devon thanked Rich as he walked him out. Then he sat on the front porch to still himself and pray before calling his parents. Devon ministered to many hurt people in his career. Still, he recognized he needed a different level of anointing to mend the hurt within his own family. He called his dad, and after explaining everything that transpired and how the charges were dropped, he broke the news about Donté. He shared how Daria spotted Donté on the streets of Charlotte and that even she did not recognize it was not him until she got closer. He shared the excitement about Donté being very much alive and living in Charlotte. Unfortunately, he also shared that Donté was currently locked up. His parents could not believe what they were hearing. Tears of sadness and joy raced down their faces. Before he finished the call, he also shared with them what Rich had told him. "He is a very hurt man. He thinks we abandoned him and did not fight hard enough to find him." There

237

was not much more to be said. They all agreed that God would have to intervene to mend their family.

Devon's mother pointed out how God had already intervened. "This entire situation brought us back together. Now we must trust God to mend hearts and open minds. We must move as He instructs us to move. I do not believe He brought Donté back into our lives to not reunite with him."

A few days after the call, Devon's parents threw some items into their suitcase, stopped by the Hendrix's to pick up their grandchildren, and drove from Smithfield, Virginia, to Charlotte. This would be a reunion like none they had ever experienced before. Pastor Royce said a prayer before he started his journey. He needed to make sure God was in the midst of this reunion and hearts were not callous. They had done all they could to find their son but were unsuccessful. How can you explain to your child that after an extended period, he was presumed dead? The police told them back then, the odds of him still being alive were little to none. Only God could set the path of restoration and forgiveness. Pastor Royce could not wait eighteen months to lay eyes on the son he thought was dead. He was determined to visit him in jail to tell him how much he was loved and missed.

Chapter 20

$\mathcal{T}$hree months had passed since the accusations were dropped against Pastor Devon. His reunion with his twin brother had an uneasy start. It was difficult to visit him in prison, but he and his father made every effort to do so. With time and prayer, he and his family were slowly rebuilding their once-broken family. Devon and Donté were intentional about reconnecting and sharing the joys and sorrows which were once empty pages of their lives. Devon would visit twice a month. So many years were lost, but God was beginning to restore the years the locust worm had destroyed. Donté was not a very spiritual person but acknowledged there had to be a greater force at work to reunite his family after all this time. Clearly, he made no promises but left it open about visiting Faith Hope and Love Church once he was released. He also agreed to receive the forgiveness offered by his mother and father. He understood accepting forgiveness was both healing for him as well as for them.

Devon could not be more excited about the progress being made. He witnessed a beautiful transformation in his family, a void being filled. It was rough and did not come with its own share of valleys, but Devon could feel the restoration...and sense the healing. He was equally excited because Rich followed through on his promise and got Donté's sentence reduced to eight months instead of eighteen. With good behavior, he could get out in six. God was working in Donté's life even if he could not see it. Devon knew once the seeds were planted, God would handle the rest.

Today was an amazing day for the Royce family. They were dedicating their son Isaiah to the Lord. This was an extra special dedication as this was the first time the whole family (except for Donté) had been together. Daria kept Tasha in the loop throughout the entire ordeal. She was already in town and could not wait to be a part of the festivities. Besides, Tasha really wanted to meet Devon's twin. She was determined to make another trip once he was released. The whole situation was like a box office thriller. The Royces and the Hendrixes drove in for the weekend to witness their grandson's dedication. But more importantly, they had a greater affinity towards spending time with family. Time was precious, and they vowed to make every opportunity to be present as often as possible.

After an anointed service and a sentimental baby dedication, they went into the fellowship hall for a delicious, bountiful meal prepared by the hospitality staff. Everyone was invited, and it felt like an old-school church homecoming. Spirits ran high, and hearts were full. Daria looked around the room and smiled. 'This is how people do ministry and life together,' she thought.

"Excuse me, everyone," Pastor Devon said as he addressed the congregation. "My heart is full today. There are no words to thoroughly convey my gratitude and love for each one of you. Church, we have been through the storm," everyone laughed. "But we made it! We may have lost a few members along the way, but let's not count them as losses. Let's just say God had some pruning to do, and He will get His work done by any means necessary," more laughter from the attendees. "Thank you for standing by my family and me. Thank you for believing the God that is in me."

He then turned to face Brother Lucas sitting at a nearby table. "Brother Lucas, I know we have not seen eye to eye. I also know you have been passionate about your convictions concerning me. Still, I thank you for remaining faithful to God despite everything. I must apologize publicly for thinking you had anything to do with the accusations being hurled my way. I know now it was just a coincidence that your relatives were the witnesses, but if my wife couldn't tell us apart, how on earth could I expect anyone else to?"

Daria tugged on Devon's arm and gave him a not-so-amused look.

"Pastor, let me help get you out of your next storm," Brother Lucas laughed as he, too, saw the look given by Lady Daria. "Now we all know I may not be your biggest fan, but I admire how you weathered this storm," Brother Lucas responded. "You showed me your character. You are a good man," Brother Lucas stood up and walked towards Pastor Devon. As he extended his hand for a handshake, he whispered to Pastor Devon, I am so sorry for listening to my family and believing the worse of you.

I am also sorry for spreading the lie throughout the congregation."

"No apologies needed. Considering the circumstances, I could have easily drawn the same conclusions had the roles been reversed," Pastor Devon assured. Turning back to the crowd, he announced, "I want to publicly acknowledge my intentions to ordain you as a church deacon. An honor which has been long overdue."

The crowd cheered. Brother Lucas placed his hand to his heart and gave a slight bow to show appreciation.

Devon then turned to his beautiful wife. "Daria, thank you for believing in me. I didn't think I could love you anymore, but God elevates my love for you each day."

Daria blushed as she returned a loving gaze to her husband.

"Last thing, and I will let you all get back to this amazing food," Pastor Devon addressed the congregation once more while trying to hold back tears wailing up in his eyes. "I don't know what I did to deserve so much love. Thank you!" Words began to stick in his throat as he tried not to release the tears which were on the precipice of streaming down his face.

Seeing how emotional her husband was, Daria stood up. "What he is trying to say," Daria smiled, "we could not have gotten through any of this without the love, prayers, and support of our natural and spiritual family."

Shouts of "We love you" rang throughout the crowd.

Tasha stood beside her best friend and gave her a loving hug. "You never cease to amaze me with your strength, courage, and longsuffering. Look around. You are an inspiration to us all. Both of you are. You guys inspire so many people. Thank you for being my family."

Devon joined the ladies in their embrace. "We love you, big head," he said as they all laughed.

****

Later that day, Joshua and Stephanie invited who they affectionately called "The Team" and their families back to the cottage. Sister Treva, Deacon Maurice, Sister Angelique, and Attorney Rich. Of course, Tasha felt like an honorary member of the team, so she was also invited. The last few months had been challenging, but in a beautiful way, they had also been a blessing. God established relationships that would last a lifetime. Devon could not help but marvel at what God had done. He took what could have been an earth-shattering situation and gained the glory from it. Not only was Devon reunited with his twin brother, but God made connections that may not have developed had he not gone through this harrowing ordeal. Souls were being saved.

Devon was particularly amazed at the assignments God birthed in his wife, Daria. Who could have known the evil man that sexually assaulted Daria as a teenager would be in the same courtroom on the same day as his bail hearing? Who knew Daria would connect with his latest victim and become her mentor and friend? Who knew the family who lost their daughter and grandchild in such a heinous way would become church members? Who knew through it all, God would birth the new Ruth's Promise ministry. This ministry uplifts and fortifies women through sharing challenges and triumphs. Never had he been more certain God's ways were not man's ways, and God's thoughts were not man's thoughts. There is no understanding Him. Devon and Daria were simply grateful God remained on their side.

As Devon looked around the room, he saw the love of God in his wife, parents, children, and spiritual family and friends. He turned to his father, "Dad, this whole situation reminds me of one of our favorite scriptures. Isaiah 40:28-31."

"Have you not known? Have you not heard? The everlasting God, the Lord, The Creator of the ends of the earth, Neither faints nor is weary. His understanding is unsearchable. He gives power to the weak, And to those who have no might He increases strength. Even the youths shall faint and be weary, And the young men shall utterly fall, But those who wait on the Lord Shall renew their strength; They shall mount up with wings like eagles, They shall run and not be weary, They shall walk and not faint."

"God is so good!" Devon's father interjected, "It's just like Him to turn tragedy into triumph!"

"Amen!" the team cheered, "Amen!"

About the
Author

ℳinister Debbie L. Reid is a wife, a mother, an ordained pastor, an author, and an entrepreneur. She is certified in several victim advocacy programs and works with various charitable organizations within her community. Minister Debb's love for Christ and passion for people fuels her desire to reach the broken and downtrodden through encouragement, ministry, counseling, and LOVE. Her dream is for her writings to build and restore hope to the hearts of people of all ages, nationalities, and genders. Although pain knows no boundaries, she truly believes that love conquerors all.

If you would like to read other titles by this author, visit her website, www.mindebb.com.

All Titles by Minister Debbie Reid:

Train Our Hands to War

Shedding Silent Tears (1st book in the Daria Hendrix series)

Life Ever Altered (2nd book in the Daria Hendrix series)

WWW.MINDEBB.COM

SUBSCRIBE TO OUR YOUTUBE CHANNEL AND WEBSITE